Room 822

"Hey... wake up, Zenrachi," a saintly voice called out. Zenrachi slowly awoke, still groggy and wiping his eyes. "HEY, JACKASS! WAKE UP!" A sudden flurry of punches to his face woke him far more quickly.

"AGHHHHHH!"

"We don't have all day. You were out for quite a while," Allura said, the pointed heels of her shoes clicking on the hard floor toward him.

"What? Where are we? And what happened to my cloak?" *Oh... right...* He groaned from the pain radiating up his body, catching sight of his pants and above them, the bandages wrapped around his midsection. He sat up on the edge of

1

the bed as his eyes adjusted, keeping his stoic demeanor.

"Ugh, you were much better asleep. Put this on. You're in a Tsurasu safe house. I'll explain the rest on the way. You should be able to move now without too much pain. Nasty wound, that was…" She tossed Zenrachi a dark, hooded cloak to veil his long grey hair, long-sleeved shirt and his shoes. He sat on the edge of the bed, glancing at his surroundings and trying to collect his thoughts as he dressed. "Let's go." The Contessa tilted her head back, leveling her blunt scowl at him as she opened the door.

The brisk air filled his lungs as they left, and Zenrachi gazed up at the sky for a moment. Something about the gray and cloudy sky calmed him, slowing his thoughts.

"What is it?" Allura turned to him suddenly.

"Besides the huge gash in my side? Nothing much. The lights, the commotion." Zenrachi gestured at the throngs of people going about their business, the numerous shops, inns, bars and brothels surrounding them, all teeming with customers. "The tall buildings.

We're in Akibara."

"No shit. Well, you still have your memory," Allura sighed, rolling her eyes. "Splendid."

"Our destination is a popular inn of some sort, correct?" Zenrachi asked, ignoring the sarcasm.

"Yes. We're to recover a necklace but more importantly, its charm – supposedly one of the stones of legend – at an event tomorrow evening. Speaking of which, there's a silver statue that stands at the inn's entrance. You can't miss it. We meet back here when all's said and done. Right. Ready?"

"W-wait! Allura!" Zenrachi began waving his hands.

"What is it?"

"Well, I'm a member of the Tsurasu now. Aren't there any rules or an initiation or something?"

"Hm… good question, dear."

"How professional." Zenrachi snorted, still concerned but not willing to show it.

"Oh, right, just one thing." Allura took a few steps forward until they stood eye to eye. "To be a member of the Tsurasu means to pursue the god within you, the one of your universe and not those passed down from history. To soar to a greater form of yourself. Nothing must lead you astray from our path. No bond, no regret, no greed and no love shall weaken our resolve as we make fate our own and look down upon this land as gods, just as they once looked down upon us. *This will be your reminder of that.*" She held her hand, revealing a silver ring. A jade gleamed at its center. "Index finger," Contessa cut in when Zenrachi made as though to speak. The ring fit his finger perfectly. He paused for a moment, staring at the ominous symbol at its center. "Yours means wandering. And mine, *human nature*," the Contessa said, flashing the blood-orange glint on her own index finger.

"Fitting." Zenrachi uttered.

"Isn't it?" She gazed at it, and Zenrachi was reminded again of her power, unmatched by anyone he knew.

They continued walking the Akibara streets, eventually coming to a corner across from a huge building. As they walked up the small set of stairs, pushing their way the masses of people, they passed a statue of the deity storm bird Horiau in front of the inn.

"Now… shall we begin? Perhaps starting with this." Allura reached behind her, pulling her sword from the sheath on her back.

"Wait, wait, wait!" Zenrachi hissed urgently as the familiar green aura surrounded her other hand.

"Ugh, what is it now?" She threw up her hands impatiently.

"What exactly are you about to do?"

"Take the necklace this inn holds and burn it down in beautiful flames, of course. What else?"

"You don't think there's a better way to go about this?" Zenrachi pleaded.

"Better than beautiful destruction? No, dear, I don't," she said bluntly.

"Look, how about we *don't* leave the hotel in flames? A more inconspicuous approach would be far less hassle. The necklace won't be going anywhere until tomorrow night. We don't even know where it is in here."

Allura sighed but looked like she was considering his proposition, darting her eyes back and forth as she pondered. "Hmph. Oh, fine, we'll go with your plan – for now," she murmured, making her own opinion clear.

"Once in there we'll need a disguise of some sort to blend in. We stick out in these cloaks." Zenrachi held out a fold of the one he was wearing, looking down at it. "We can't look as though we're up to something." The Contessa only huffed in reply, clearly still displeased, and they continued on in silence.

The two strode the narrow ways of Akibara the next evening, lined with houses and shops. Approaching the base of the tall buildings and brightly-colored signs was like entering a different realm, and the Contessa nudged him as they reached their rendezvous point. The silver statue outside of the inn gleamed brightly as they walked into the lobby, and seeing a man and woman ahead of them walking off to the restrooms on the side corridor, Zenrachi and Allura shared a brisk nod of understanding. The training he had received since childhood served Zenrachi well, allowing him to quickly adapt to opportunities as they presented themselves.

He emerged from the restroom only a few moments later, still adjusting the suit properly. Nearby in the women's restroom he heard a sharp cry, quickly cut off and followed immediately by a loud thud. Walking in, he saw blood running down one of the tiled walls as Allura emerged from the stall, now changed into a red dress. More blood dripped from her sharply pointed nails.

"I might have gotten a bit too excited," Allura grinned as she slipped on a pair of sunglasses and washed the blood from her hands. Zenrachi grimaced but said nothing as they proceeded on toward the reception desk. "I'll take care of this," she said, radiating confidence. "Watch and learn."

They moved through the crowd of people as the reception desk appeared from between them.

"Hello! Welcome to our resort!" the receptionist said "How may I help you two today?"

"We're supposed to be on the guest list for the event here tomorrow. You see, my... *husband* and I are running terribly late, and need a room arranged. That wouldn't be too much of a problem..." Allura inched closer, lowering the sunglasses to reveal her gleaming emerald eyes. "... Now would it?" she finished sweetly.

The receptionist's eyes dulled, her smile now frozen in place. "Not at all. Just a moment." Her voice came slowly, the words spoken with a dreamlike quality. She handed Allura a room key and passes for the event. "Enjoy your stay, madam."

"Nice plan, dear. I think I'm starting to like this," Allura smirked at Zenrachi as she took the keys to their suite. "Up those stairs, our room is on the eighth floor. And carry my bag for me, will you, dear?"

"Your bag? When did you get a ba-"

"Come now, Zenrachi, it's a long way up." She cut him off, shoving a bag into his arms, and was already halfway up the stairs before Zenrachi could follow, leaving him to trail behind.

She had disappeared from sight by the time Zenrachi reached the top of the stairwell and found their room. He turned the handle and the Contessa once again emerged seemingly from thin air beside him, startling him back a step. "Took you long enough," she said, turning the key and throwing open the door to reveal their suite.

Still uneasy, Zenrachi spared no time in putting a little distance between them as they entered the empty suite. Someone as unpredictable as the Contessa made him nervous, and she had nearly killed him once already. He entered another room leading off from the entrance and immediately noticed something sitting on the bed – a robe, neatly folded, and much more to his taste than what he currently wore. *Good, a kimono. I could use something other than this ill-fitting thing.* He hastily changed into the robe, tossing the suit to the floor in distaste. Then he lay on the bed, staring at the ceiling and quickly losing himself in deep thought. *How did I get myself into this? And alongside this… woman no less.* His eyes slipped closed.

Awaking after a few hours of sleep, Zenrachi emerged from his room, walking into the kitchen area to find Allura rummaging through the cupboards.

"Ahh! Just what I was looking for." She pulled out a glass whiskey bottle with a yellow jacket on the label. "Perfect!" She flicked her gaze toward Zenrachi. "So what were you doing in there all this time, taking a snooze?" She tipped the bottle to her lips, swigging the liquid and closing her eyes in appreciation.

"Well, after waking up in bandages just yesterday with no clue where I was, then realizing I was stuck with the same person who very nearly killed me, yeah, now that you mention it, I could use some rest."

Allura appeared to ponder for a moment, staring at him. "Here. You'd think they'd keep things like this out of plain view." She handed him a large piece of paper. "Schematics of the entire place."

"How did you get this?"

Allura grinned. "You really want to know?"

The Contessa perched on the chandelier above a mass of guards in the large hall of the hotel. The vantage point offered her a clear view of the balcony and the rest of the hall, occupied by a number of swordsmen.

"Well, well," she muttered to herself. "This isn't typical staff security. Time to blow off some steam." She surveyed the hall, eyeing her targets – her prey. One swordsman lurked in the shadows away from the rest, and she pounced before he could even catch sight of her, let alone lift his sword to defend himself. She hit the ground as softly as a cat, her own blade having already pierced his jugular. He died before he had the strength to cry out, the blood pooling around him, and she snatched back the blade from his corpse, not bothering to wipe it clean before sheathing it again. Emerging from the shadows, she was spotted by another guardsman.

"You must be lost. This is a restricted area, you need to leave immediately," the guard barked out, his superior height towering over her.

"Why, yes... you're quite right, we wouldn't want anybody getting hurt, now would we?" She brushed her hand across his cheek. It was a long fall from the balcony, she noted, and the thought made her smile widen. The cold, hard

ground would be there to break his fall. Her gaze sharpened, and her eyes gleamed as his grew suddenly dull.

He turned from her and approached the balcony. She watched a brief, internal struggle cross his face, his mouth twitching as it sought to force some words out before his mind surrendered to the inevitable. Two other guards, seeing his movements, ran to him and attempted to restrain him, but their efforts were in vain. The balcony railing simply crumbled away beneath them, and two of the three men fell swiftly to their deaths. The last was left peering over the broken railing, and others quickly converged upon the damage with shouts of alarm.

A ray of green light appeared from Allura's fingertips, and there was a loud explosion that sent several more guards flying from the balcony. One final guardsman gripped his sword in fear. Her gaze met his darting eyes. It took only a stare to restrict his movements completely, and the clicking of her heels grew louder as she approached, the guard struggling desperately to move against invisible bonds. Her blade sunk through his chest before he could scream, a pool of blood quickly forming as his life dwindled away in front of her eyes.

Allura licked her lips. "With your final mortal breath, behold the eyes of Aidoku. Pray that your fate in the afterlife differs from this one." His mouth formed another silent scream as her deadly green orb shot from her hand, throwing him from the balcony to his death.

The Contessa whipped her sword through the air, flicking the blood from it before walking over to a table in one corner of the room, where papers lay scattered across its surface. She paused for a moment, surveying the wall for a diagram of the inn building. "Aha!" Snatching up the piece of paper, Allura exited the hall, to return to a no doubt still slumbering Zenrachi in the suite a few floors up.

"So, while you were *sleeping*, I took care of a few things we'll need… since we're not just leaving the place in ashes like I'd originally planned," Allura smirked, finishing the story. "Don't forget, this was your idea, after all. The auction is tomorrow evening. Afterward, there'll be a party for all the patrons who attended. That will be our opportunity to take the jewel. Now. A drink?" She extended the bottle to Zenrachi.

"… No thanks," Zenrachi shook his head, feeling another prickling of unease at her calm, despite the fact that here and there, tiny droplets of blood still freckled her face.

"Hmph. You're no fun. So be it, more for me." Allura took another swig from the bottle. Then she cocked her head, regarding him coolly. "So you're supposedly Dentori's lost one, a savant of the martial arts."

Zenrachi scowled, this time accepting the bottle as she extended it toward him. "A martial artist?" he scoffed. "I'm no fighter. Not anymore." He poured a generous amount of the whiskey into a glass, and a loud thunk punctuated his words as he downed it and slammed it back onto the table.

"It was right around the time your brother, Seijin, was killed, igniting the coup, breaking the pact of peace in Arashi Tochi and leaving the nations in disarray. Which is what the Tsurasu is for. Order and true justice…" Allura's eyes did not leave Zenrachi's face as she took another swig.

It was Zenrachi who broke the awkward silence first. "Those eyes…what do you truly see, Allura?"

"It's Contessa," she reminded him, narrowing her eyes. "And in front of me, all I see is once-mighty armor with an immense crack running through it." Zenrachi shifted uncomfortably as Allura continued. "But what is very real in our future is the revival of the storm god… and justice by my hand."

"… Nice to know where I stand," Zenrachi finally spoke, unable to keep the nervousness from his voice. "You've already tried to kill me, and did who knows what to me while I was unconscious. And all I know is your name."

Allura shrugged carelessly. "Perhaps I got a little excited after I finally got the fighter in you to come out and play. You can hardly blame me, can you?" She flashed a predatory grin. "You should be grateful. Not only did I keep you alive, but you're the first to survive my beautiful cluster of explosions." She got up and began to circle Zenrachi, unblinking. "Besides, it's not like you bothered to check before. You can know anything you want to, dear. All you have to do… is ask." She grabbed the bottle from the table and walked away, leaving Zenrachi alone in bewildered silence.

Still exhausted and recovering from his wounds, Zenrachi slept again, and emerged from his rooms as the shadows were growing longer. He walks outside to the balcony to find Allura leaning against the railing, smoking an odd-smelling cigar. Like him, she had now changed into a kimono, and he couldn't help but gaze at her in the luminous moonlight.

"So, you're up? What is it, dear – got lonely without me?" She exhaled a cloud of smoke.

"Those eyes of yours. You used them on the woman at the reception desk."

"Intriguing, aren't they? My eyes hold a special ability that can turn anyone into my puppet with just a look… or stop a powerful opponent in my line of sight dead in their tracks for a split second, which is more than enough for me. I didn't get the name Contessa for nothing." She offered Zenrachi the cigar.

"I don't smo-"

"It's not what you think. It's a healing herb grown in the land of Bofu." She winked. "Trust me. Would I ever lie?"

"Yes," Zenrachi said flatly. Then he sighed. "You make it sound so easy. Fine. Give it here." Zenrachi inhaled, taking in the earthly smell, then put the cigar to his mouth and breathed in deeply. "I… see," he said, coughing. "And what about your explosives?" he continued. "And these marks on your wrists?" He reached toward her, pulling one of her kimono sleeves up to reveal the markings snaking around her wrist. "Did you use these to summon your divine fireworks? The same ones you nearly killed me with them before we arrived here?"

The corners of Allura's mouth tilted upward. "Ah ah ah, the Contessa does not kiss and tell. So. Feeling it yet?" She pointed to the cigar in his hand, raising an eyebrow.

Zenrachi looked out over the city, feeling the night wind from the balcony rustling through his hair. "It feels… peaceful, like my body is finally at ease. A strange herb this is."

"Some say it's an escape from the pain, stress and despair that makes up their life."

"Is there truly an escape from such things?" Zenrachi asked, a note of bitterness creeping into his voice.

"Ah, you're learning. Good. However, it doesn't hurt to indulge a bit and let your mind wander. And it heals the body through this from of consumption." She took the cigar back from him, stabbing it out before beginning to walk back into the suite.

"What about tomorrow? You have a plan, don't you?"

"I do, as it happens." She smiled as she glanced back at him, rousing his suspicions, but said no more as the silence stretched out between them.

Finally he could not bear the curiosity. "Well?"

"Let's just say that I hope that you can dance as well as you can fight… Zenrachi." The glass door slid closed behind her, her brilliant red hair the last thing to disappear from his sight.

Zenrachi slept fitfully that night, awakening again suddenly when it was still pitch black. He waited for his eyes to adjust, then crept out of his room to check on Allura, hearing her snores as he approached. Peering over, he saw Allura sound asleep on the couch, her arm hanging out of her covers and holding the same whiskey bottle as before.

"I guess there's something that can even put her down," he whispered to himself.

"But what is very real in our future is the revival of the storm god… and justice by my hand…" Her words replayed in his head, sending chills down his spine.

"She can't find out," Zenrachi hissed, clenching his fists. "This power could bring *my* light back, unlock its true power… and it may be the key to discovering the truth of what made Allura who she is…"

A Deadly Rhythm

A loud banging on the door served as a rude awakening the next morning. It was still early, and Zenrachi jumped to his feet and emerged from his room, seeing the Contessa leaning against the wall. Her grip was tight on her sword, and her eyes shot up as he entered the room.

"Shhh." She put a finger to her lips and signaled him over to the door.

He crept forward so that they were facing each other on either side of the door. When Zenrachi had positioned himself, the Contessa slowly unlocked it and they both prepared to strike.

The door suddenly shot open, slamming Zenrachi behind it. A small elderly woman walked through, casually waving off Allura's drawn blade. "Finally, you two are up. You're late for your appointment," she snapped.

The Contessa gazed at the elderly woman in confusion. "What appointm-"

"You, come here." The woman gestured at Allura impetuously, completely ignoring the weapon still pointed in her direction. "We can get started immediately. Wait, wait, I have a tuxedo for the man. Where is he?" The front door slid back from the wall, revealing Zenrachi holding his head and grimacing in pain. "Ah, there you are. Your tuxedo is in that bag. Now get dressed, I'll have this young lady here done in about twenty minutes."

"What are you–"

Still ignoring her words, the women grabbed a lock of the Contessa's hair, pulling it toward her. "Let's see here, nice shoulders, tight curves…"

"HEY!" The Contessa shrieked as she was grabbed by the hip.

"Hair a bit on the wild side, nothing I can't fix, of course." The older woman unzipped the large black bag, revealing a gleaming crimson dress. "This should go perfectly with your skin tone."

"But who *are* you, and why-"

"You hired me, remember? Two artists who hired the best stylist Akibara has to offer need to make a splash at this event. Now, get dressed, quickly! Goodness, spend one night in the city and you lose all sense," she grumbled. Zenrachi and Allura's eyes met, Zenrachi shrugging his shoulders, and he quickly left her to the old woman's mercies as he disappeared to change.

The time of the event approached. Zenrachi stood near the central staircase leading to the ballroom, still awaiting Allura. He stayed near the crowds in an effort to blend in, although the noise of constant chatter set him on edge. "Dammit, that old woman said twenty minutes, what's taking so long?" he muttered to himself. At that moment, he heard the click of heels approach from behind him and turned – and was immediately stunned at the appearance of Allura descending the staircase. She wore a crimson dress cut in the traditional fashion, slit at either side to reveal a wide expanse of each leg. Realizing he was staring, Zenrachi blinked and shook his head.

The Contessa did not seem to notice. "Ugh, the sooner I can get out of this thing, the better." She continued toward him, fidgeting with the sash around her waist that shaped the dress tightly around her hips. Finally, now only inches away, she looked at Zenrachi, flushing slightly. "And when you're done staring we can get this over with!" she said, her voice rising to a near-shout. She brushed roughly past him, proceeding to the ballroom entrance. It was decorated elegantly and hung with bright lights all around it, illuminating the floor now crowded with guests.

"Remember, this was your idea," the Contessa whispered as she wrapped her arm around Zenrachi's. They made their way to their assigned table as they observed the guests around them. "Celebrated guests, what scum. The ministers, police, officials, gang leaders, the wealthy… *they're* the ones with the most blood on their hands.

They're what people like us are for. To cleanse this world of its blemishes to make our perfect utopia. Their time will come," Allura said, grinding her teeth in irritation. "Zenrachi, bring me a drink. Preferably something dark."

Zenrachi rose and walked up to the bar, happy to take the chance to gain some distance from her. *She's too unpredictable*, he thought to himself. *That look… she's up to something.* As he made his way through the crowds, he saw someone approach from the corner of his eye. An arm shot out, quickly pulling him to the side and away from the nearby crowds. Zenrachi regained his footing and stared. A pair of eyes in front of him stared back at him.

"Zen…rachi?"

It was the first time he had seen her since his exodus from Dentori. "Aurecala!"

"Enenki… live in the flesh." Cala's eyes were still widened in surprise. "Where on earth have you been all this time?" And then, as the Contessa crept up to stand beside Zenrachi, making him jump: "And who is *she*?"

"Hmm, good question. For the next several hours, at least… his wife." The Contessa smirked, not bothering to hide her malicious intent. "An old friend, Zenrachi dear?" She extended her hand toward Cala.

"Pleasure to meet you." Cala did not reach out a hand in response, and her eyes had narrowed in suspicion. "So… here on honeymoon, are we?"

"We have business here," the Contessa purred. "And what brings Dentori's best huntress to a venue such as this?"

Cala sniffed, her disdain obvious. "I'm hoping to run into a certain someone. As well as a sacred necklace from the several that were auctioned earlier tonight."

"… Sorry, dear, we must really be going. It was a pleasure meeting you." The Contessa grabbed Zenrachi suddenly by the arm, bringing an abrupt end to the pleasantries.

"What was that about?" Zenrachi asked, confused at the sudden shift. His arm was still held by the Contessa tightly, and he fought to release her grip.

"It's become apparent that we're not the only ones who came for the jewelry."

They had walked the length of the floor, and at the front of the ballroom stood another statue of the storm god Horiau, the necklace around its neck facing the guests. Its massive wings were extended outward, displaying more jewels on the feathers of its silver-plated wings.

"It's almost midnight, what is she waiting for?" Zenrachi whispered to himself, glancing over his shoulder at the Contessa.

"You say something?"

"You never told me exactly how we're supposed to get this necklace off the statue's neck and out of this room full of people, back to the hideout."

"It's simple, dear. We wait they've had plenty to drink, like right about now, and we give them a show they can't take their eyes from." She grinned, eyeing him up and down.

"You mean... a dance? You were serious?" Zenrachi yelped.

"You're the one who suggested taking a 'low key' approach if I remember correctly. Relax, dear, I don't bite. You already managed to survive our first duet, after all." Her smirk grew wider. "Here, take the lead." She offered him her hand. "And be sure to approach the center of the crowd," she said in a lower voice. "Let's see if you've got rhythm, *warrior*. I'll follow your lead." To the sounds of the music now beginning, Zenrachi and the Contessa started to dance.

They were among the first to begin, and the noise from the people around them grew. The Contessa was skillful and light on her feet, Zenrachi striving to match her movements, and their dancing attracted plenty of admiring glances and murmurs. As they gained the crowd's attention, freeing her hand clutched inside Zenrachi's, the Contessa weaved a discreet sign in the air, silently summoning her double. As they continued to dance, keeping the eyes of crowd firmly rooted on them, the Contessa's doppelganger emerged from thin air near the side of the room, sneaking over to unhook the necklace from the bird's neck. As the music ended, Zenrachi and the Contessa still holding one another in a dramatic pose, the crowd applauded wildly. The Contessa inched closer until little more than a breath separated them.

"Time for our curtain call…" she whispered, the words tickling past his ear. An instant later, her doppelganger turned her hand palm up, a green aura emitting from her hand. Expressionless, she launched her explosive sphere at the colossal statue standing at the front of the ballroom.

Zenrachi gasped. "What are you doing?" he whispered frantically.

"Shall we, dear? The curtain is about to fall on this act," came the Contessa's only reply.

Her doppelganger's explosive bombarded the statue, causing it to crumble over the ballroom floor and a wall of flames to burst up, creating a smokescreen that slowly engulfed the room. As Zenrachi looked back, he saw that Allura had disappeared from his side.

Searching for an escape from the screams and sudden rush of people, an immense surge of light suddenly rushed into Zenrachi's head. His vision became blurred and lightning flashed in front of his eyes, disorientating him. He fell to his knees as the frantic crowd ran past. His distorted vision revealed two shadows approaching him, although he could only see them in brief flashes. Distant laughter echoed in his mind for what felt like hours until the illusion finally subsided, the jostling and commotion of the crowd snapping him suddenly back to his senses.

Zenrachi looked up to see the fiery ballroom around him and quickly rose to his feet, making his way to the side stairwell. From there he reached the streets of Akibara, fleeing the smoke and still screaming crowd. Once outside he continued to walk, avoiding eye contact with anyone, eager to avoid undue attention. Striving for calm, he moved through the darkened streets, knowing he now needed to make it back to the rendezvous point near the house where he had first awakened. He did not notice that someone had been watching him the entire time.

As he walked, something emerged from the shadows and wrapped a hand over his mouth before he could utter a single word, dragging him into one of the many alleyways running between the tall buildings. In front of him appeared a shadowy figure holding a blade to his neck.

"Will this be your last dance?" a familiar voice said. "That woman is wanted all across the land of storms. And now *you're her new partner in crime?* You have no idea who you're getting involved with... Enenki."

"Aurecala." Zenrachi's eyes narrowed. "The only crime I've committed is not giving that audience an encore."

"You haven't done anything... yet. This path of vengeance or whatever it is must stop. It will only drive you to madness. You aren't the Zenrachi I've fought countless times, the one I fought alongside... and the one I once loved."

"No. I'm not little Zenrachi miserable from what this life's given him. I'm the Zenrachi who's seen the darkness, the truth of this land and this life. And I'll be the one you'll one day thank for my deeds, done to mold this world into the Arashi Tochi it once was." Zenrachi was only dimly aware that he was speaking. His mouth seemed to move of its own will as the anger in his mind grew. "You, along with what's left of Dentori, hiding behind those walls that protect your home, praying to some fictional deity and hoping things won't revert back to their violent past. I'm not on the opposing side of you – I'm simply the two storms of good... and evil."

Cala slowly lowered her blade, and Zenrachi turned sharply to walk away.

"Zen! Stop-" Thunder cracked through the air as Cala made to grab him. The storm bird appeared in a flash in her mind. By the time her vision returned, Zenrachi had vanished from the dark alley.

After escaping Cala, Dentori's bounty hunter, Zenrachi continued on to the agreed upon spot near the house, far away from the destruction of the ballroom. It was now long past midnight, although Zenrachi had no way of knowing how much time had passed. As he reached for the door, he felt a gaze upon him from a nearby shop and looked around, spotting the Contessa lifting sunglasses back over her eyes as she lifted the shop's banner. Cautious, he approached the red-haired woman who had long since escaped the blazing ballroom.

"There you are, dear. I was beginning to think you stood me up."

"Drop the damn act. What the hell was that back there? We'd already gotten what we came for." He took a seat across from her, scowling.

"You just don't see the big picture yet. You naïve boy." She heaved a sigh, shaking her head. "This is only the beginning. To attain ancient power, revive the deities, is just the start to what will be a momentous end… Oh, and another thing, dear," said the Contessa as a blade came whistling down, stabbing right through his hand to the table. "Next time you run off again, you're an assumed rouge. Remember this, and remember it well. If you're not with us, you're against us, and then I'll have to come get you myself." She bent down to whisper in his ear, their cheeks brushing. "And trust me… you don't want that."

"You're a madwoman!" Zenrachi shouted in pain, his hand pinned to the table.

A waitress approached their booth, seemingly unfazed by the situation. Her smile was vacant. "Your order is ready, madam. And what can I get for you?" she asked emotionlessly, turning to Zenrachi.

Zenrachi paused, realizing that something wasn't right with the waitress standing before him. She was under the Contessa's control then. He played along and fought to remain calm, even with a blade embedded in his hand. "Green tea." He took a sharp breath, then yanked the knife from his hand as Allura began slurping her noodles noisily.

"Sorry about that, I can be quite irritable when I get hungry," Allura said sweetly, mouth full. "Here." She offered him a plate from the platter to Zenrachi.

"Don't really have an appetite," Zenrachi replied, his hand now bleeding profusely. "Long day." With impeccable timing, his stomach gave a loud growl.

"Just take it." Allura let out a sigh as she slid the large plate toward him.

"So… what now?" Zenrachi asked, still holding his wounded hand.

"We simply wait for whoever they sent to take the necklace off our hands."

As if on cue, the door to the small shop opened. Several men in suits like the one Zenrachi wore walked in, followed by a familiar face behind them. The men surrounded the booth.

"Let me do the talking," Allura instructed in a low tone.

A bulky man with slicked back blonde hair emerged from the crowd of men that circled them. He stood smaller in comparison to the others, but very stout. He looked right at Zenrachi, gifting him with a menacing stare.

"Enenki," he said in a gravely tone, evidently recognizing him from their time in Dentori. "There's been a change of plan. You two are off of the hook for now, seeing as I have things under control here in Akibara. Yogen is pleased with your acquisition."

"Guess you found a way to be the big man, huh Sakumo?" Zenrachi asked, a grin on his face that he knew was sure to antagonize the other man.

"How about I knock you down a couple of notches yourself," came the immediate threat.

"Both of you, stop talking, right now. If you have everything covered here then take the damn jewelry to Yogen at once," Allura said to Sakumo, glaring. "And just for pissing me off, I'll be taking some extra on top of what I'm owed."

Sakumo glared back, but gestured toward one of his men, who reached into his suit pocket and pulled out a large amount of cash. Sakumo took it, placing it on the table and leaving without a word, his men following suit.

Allura snapped her head back to Zenrachi, staring him down.

"I told you to be quiet. But you just couldn't resist, could you. Old 'friends', I assume? Too bad he won't be here much longer."

Zenrachi narrowed his eyes. "What are you saying?"

"Just that he's reckless. Nothing more than paid muscle, a drug mover in the underworld of Akibara who carelessly flashes his money around. Whatever potential he once showed as a fighter, he's left to rot in the clubs and gambling rings he's known in." The Contessa tossed her head, smiling now. "But anyone can be bought. Just like that group of men around him when he entered. The tables can turn quickly, especially on someone who puts themselves so foolishly out in the open. Just you watch."

The Song and the Storm

"Now. It was about time for them to be leaving. And we'll be doing the same," Allura snapped, clearly still irritated. She stood and grabbed the wad of cash as Zenrachi followed, picking up the loose bills and leaving them on the table.

They walked deeper into Akibara. The streets were lively despite the late hour, but Zenrachi was not used to the crowds and felt on edge. He followed as Allura turned sharply, walking into a dimly lit building.

"Are you here to burn this place down too?" he asked, sarcasm bleeding into his voice.

"Nope, just a drink of the serpent's nectar." Curious to know what she meant, Zenrachi continued to trail behind as they walked to the back of the building. Allura approached a dark-haired woman pouring drinks for two men who were sitting at the bar. "Venom on the rocks… kiddo," Allura said to the bartender.

Her eyes shot up, then the woman smiled. "The lovely but dangerous Contessa herself, back in the city… or should I say, *Leruna.*" At the sound of this, the two men looked up and hurriedly cleared out. "Should've known the earlier fireworks I heard tell of were for a special occasion," the bartender continued. She reached for two glasses and poured a liquid into them from an odd-looking vase, handing one to the Contessa and the other to Zenrachi, who seated themselves at the bar. "Hm… now where'd you find this one, Allura?"

"The lost warrior of Dentori himself," Allura replied, smirking.

"I knew I'd seen you before. That ashen hair. And even more handsome in person, I must say. I hope you stay on her good side so you don't end up like the rest of her-"

"Ekora. *Enough.*" Allura slammed her glass on the table, slowly wiping her lip with her finger and staring the bartender down with eyes that sparked dangerously.

"Right. Sorry," Ekora replied a little nervously, wiping down the bar with a rag. Then she reached down below the bar and handed Allura a folded-up piece of paper.

"So, what does it do?" Zenrachi inquired, breaking the awkward silence that had settled.

"Oh the stone? From my knowledge of Arashi Tochi and this intel here, the markings on two of them each resemble some kind of creature. Legend has it there are two such creatures that once existed in Arashi Tochi. Kotori, the song bird, and its counterpart, Horiau."

The Reaper of Storms. Zenrachi's eyes widened, realizing the will and the fate of Horiau lay within him.

"I will find the god of storms one day. And drive my divine sword through its heart for what it's done to me." Allura's hands clenched.

"And what will happen to the stone after it gets to Yogen?"

"Don't know, don't care." She took a gulp of her drink. "Too many different rituals with no clear one that's directly needed to revive either of those so-called 'gods'. In this day and age, the origin of how such deities and spiritual items came about is fragmented, leaving people to wonder which tale is right. Those stones are mere charms at this point. Which is why we found one at an art gallery being sold off to whoever threw enough money at it."

"In a ballroom you destroyed," Zenrachi pointed out. "What do you think happened to those people?" *Those innocent people.*

Allura heard the unspoken words and scoffed. "Those people... those who corrupt this very land and put the people you cared for through hardship just so they can kick their feet up. Whether they escaped that fire or not, they had it coming – I simply did them a favor. Coming to a city to escape the fear of their sins, their pasts coming back to haunt them, trying to wash it all away until they're so drunk they can't see straight. They deserved their fate."

"Does anyone deserve that?"

"Naïve boy." Allura looked at him, a dangerous note in her voice. "This is just what comes of trying to recreate solace. The Tsurasu shall create a world with true justice."

"So what's the Contessa's endgame?" Zenrachi asked, not sure he wanted to hear the answer.

"Once Yogen revives the storm deity, what he does with those stones makes no difference to me. I'm going to… *intervene*. Destroy the deity and end the cycle of destruction that comes with it. Where I once lived, the people lived in fear of the god of storms. Bofu was home to many skilled fighters, yet people grew so fearful of the bird's revival that they began suspecting anyone different, anyone with skills unknown to them to be the second coming of the dark storm that once tormented them long ago." Zenrachi listened in silence, fascinated, as she continued. "Among the accused were my mother and father. Her eyes were the first of their kind in that place. And my father, a skilled assassin, notorious in his time, a protector of his homelands ruler. Both were cut down in their prime from fear – fear of an accursed legend with countless interpretations, leaving moralists to endlessly wonder which was right. They were killed for *nothing*, just because people feared a god that no longer exists! But one day, the legend shall be brought to life… and then it will meet death, once and for all."

"Allura…"

She did not appear to hear him. "I live now for my art, and it shall set ablaze the bird that cursed me. I used what my parents taught me, perfecting their skills until I became the Contessa that stands before you now. *We* are the force to bring true peace, never forget that. Sacrifices must be made to reach what we truly desire. I was like you once. Lost… without light, without guidance. Cold, emotionless, left to the darkness. But soon the mighty power we must take for ourselves will emerge. In time, you'll come to understand."

"As long as you don't lose your head and try to kill me again," Zenrachi replied. Her words were harsh, but deep down he knew a part of him felt the same way.

"Don't get ahead of yourself," Allura smiled at him, and an unexpected note of fondness crept into her voice.

Zenrachi paused from his story, gazing up at the moonlit sky as his thoughts slowly returned to the present. Hisashi and Rahku had been silent, listening intently, as Zenrachi told the tale of him and the Contessa.

"… I wonder how jealous Allura was of Cala." Hisashi mused, eventually breaking the quiet.

"Don't remind me." Zenrachi glanced at the scar on his hand.

"That Contessa seems much different from the embodiment of rage Hisashi and I had the pleasure of meeting," Rahku added quietly. "Rage… carried for so long, and the thought of vengeance that drove both of you in your actions."

But the you I know is still in there — the you from the ballroom. The same you who stabbed me through the hand for being late, Zenrachi thought to himself. *How deep in your rage are you know, Allura...?*

"Zen!"

Zenrachi shook his head, startled out of his reverie at the sound of Rahku's voice.

"Zoned out there?" Hisashi asked, one eyebrow raised.

"No… its nothing."

" Ya know Zen, nothing' is beginning to be a whole lot when it comes to you, so maybe you should start letting us in on whatever it is," Rahku said.

"Oh boy," Hisashi muttered to himself as Zenrachi and Rahku stared each other down.

"You have something you want to say to me?" Zenrachi demanded.

"Between your actions and watching you get beaten to a pulp by the angry chick and your doppelganger, where would you like me to begin?" Rahku shot back.

"Maybe at the part when a lightning bird deity merged with you for starters?" Hisashi pointed out for him.

There was a long pause as Zenrachi struggled with his anger, before he exhaled deeply and the tension between them eased. "There wasn't much left for me in Dentori. Seijin's death left enough of a dark cloud over my life that I saw nothing there for me anymore. He was the only person I had left, and I was helpless to do anything about it. It left a wound that was far too deep to be healed. Yyolin-sensei wasn't the same after that either." He closed his eyes, remembering. "The day I left for good, she still wouldn't show her pain at allowing her son to leave that place. And I could only put faith in her teachings then. I didn't believe I would crash and fall to the dark storm. There was a void deep within me that couldn't be filled." He took another deep breath.

"After my exodus, I traveled the vast lands of Arashi Tochi in an effort to find my spark again, that flame that once burned within me. And to do people like you, who I still had some ties with, a favor by concealing my pain from you, seeing what truly resided in the land of storms. And as I traveled the land, it all became clearer and clearer."

"And what exactly was that?" Rahku asked, listening attentively.

"That the events that occurred that fateful day were all part of a carefully put together plan now in full motion. My brother was the arbitrary casualty that sparked the coup."

"The alliance of the four nations was supposed to prevent this." Rahku bowed his head, recognizing the reality of the very world they hoped to save, but still hoping to retrieve his friend from the void within him.

Zenrachi placed his hand on his shoulder. "Don't. For you should rejoice – the inevitable is finally beginning. The beginning of the end. Everywhere I went, I saw that evil plagued this land. Resources have become scarce and people will do anything to survive, even if that means turning on one another, revealing humankind's true foul nature. As the brightest of young martial artists either turned to the darkness or stood by their village to protect their homes, I sought out the ancient deity of our land atop Kenzai Mountain. And I found not only an answer in return, but instead an actual appearance from the very winged deity to whom I so angrily called."

Thunder Roars
Lightning Strikes

Rahku and Hisashi were silent now as Zenrachi continued to speak.

"The storm bird merged with me is both gift and curse. I had ventured around Kenzai Mountain endlessly to find the mysteries hidden at the top. I stumbled upon the cave, within which were many scriptures engraved all over its walls. Emerging from the cave to the edge of the cliff, I called out to the dark sky as heavy storm formed. Demanding answers for the fate I'd been handed, why I must have been bound to those feelings… answers for why the god of our land would allow a pure heart to become blackened, losing the love of the arts I once had. And in that instant, a huge crack of blue lightning struck and before me appeared a silver bird, shrouded in the descending storm clouds."

"So let me guess, you're actually some child of prophecy who's going to save our world, right?" Sarcasm was heavy in Hisashi's voice.

"Quite the contrary. I am no child of prophecy. Rather, I am a god of my destiny, as we all are. I, not fate, control my destiny. I took in the spirit of the storm bird and we became one. I shall soon learn to control this spirit within me too, and then shall I be an unstoppable force to anyone who tries to oppose me."

"I'm beginning to see now..." Rahku spoke quietly to himself. "That spirit is doing something to Zenrachi, changing him from the inside. It's become a mirrored version of himself that's overpowering him. But the Zenrachi I used to know is still there too, trapped within the darkness. Could those markings in the cave signify a set of trials? Is Zenrachi even the first host of the deity? What if... what if they're a warning.?" He recalled what the dark, vengeful, inner Zenrachi had said before merging with the god and vanishing completely.

"Shall the will of Horiau fall, the dark storm shall rise again."

"And where does the lovely Contessa fall into all this? How did you even meet up in the first place?" Hisashi asked.

Zenrachi looked at him, his eyes becoming focused again. "Wandering Arashi Tochi for some time, I still trained to ready myself for the day I would fight again with purpose. The months passed and I kept myself isolated, nothing more to anyone who saw me than a passing shadow. For a while, I stayed in a small village on the outskirts of the green lands of Bofu, figuring that the deep forests would be enough to stay unnoticed. Little did I know that someone had woven their threads all through that vast forest. Every day I'd go deep into the woods to train, until finally, upon returning one day, I sensed that something was off. I knew someone had been awaiting my return."

"But why target you, Zen? If you'd been a ghost…."

"Precisely. I didn't know either, and I wasn't about to call out to the shadows and ask. I crept between the trees, making my way toward the house I was staying in to try and catch a glimpse of the intruder through the cracks of the wooden roof.

"Well well, isn't someone instinctive?" The words came softly from behind him, sending a chill down Zenrachi's spine. He slowly turned as the shadows shifted and heard heels clicking on the wooden roof, catching the glint of amethyst shining in the moonlight as someone walked slowly forward. From the shadows emerged a striking woman with fiery-red hair and strange markings encircling her wrists, clad in a close-fitting cheongsam.

She pounced before Zenrachi had time to take in anything more or react. With only his close combat skills left, all he could do was try to weave around the deadly swipes of her sword. One stroke brushed his cheek, the edge of her jian sword cutting him and she grabbed hold of his jacket in the other hand and jerked him in closer. Licking the blood dripping down his cheek, her foot then dug into his rib cage, and a flying kick launched him from the roof straight to the ground below.

On his back, Zenrachi gasped in pain and saw her blade flying straight for him. He rolled out of the way just in time and sprung to his feet, wiping the blood from his face. From the sky an orb flew at him, crashing toward him before exploding on impact.

He shielded his eyes against the brightness and suddenly she appeared behind him, her palm on his back, emitting a green aura before it exploded and sent Zenrachi flying into the forest.

"But you had storm bird within you," Hisashi interrupted the tale. "Do things like that really affect you?"

"I'm a god, not an immortal," Zenrachi replied. "It hurt… a lot. Not only that, but I had no idea had to summon such power."

By the time Zenrachi had gathered his wits enough to look around him, he saw that several explosive spheres had him cornered, creating a large smokescreen as they exploded one after the other. He could only see the clouded moonlight from above, and he gazed toward the sky in despair as the orbs came crashing down.

Bit by bit, the smoke gradually cleared. Breathing frantically, Zenrachi found himself unscathed. He examined his hands, gasping at the mysterious light illuminating them. His eyes darted up, seeing a crescent ring before it quickly faded away into the moonlight.

"I had felt my life on the edge of extinction," Zenrachi spoke as Rahku and Hisashi listened intently. "My life, or what had become of it, was staring at a new face of death. And I hated that feeling. I decided then, no longer was anyone going to play with my fate. It infuriated me to feel so... useless. And at that moment, something just... awakened inside of me. My hands clenched in a blind fury as what looked like thunderbolts emerged from them. I heaved them into the smoke, and when that too finally cleared, walking toward me was the Contessa, without a scratch on her. Perhaps staring at what I had thought was my inevitable death right in the face ignited a flame within me. A woman had appeared out of nowhere, bent on taking my life, but I couldn't let everything crumble around me and die, just another lost wanderer, another victim. I was going to do the only thing I knew – fight."

Enraged, Zenrachi pounced at her in a flurry of strikes, just like he had once before, his old abilities returning to him. They traded punches until the force from so many simultaneous blows sent them tumbling away from each other, and the Contessa smirked as he looked up at her. Green orbs were stuck to his body. She clenched her hand, triggering their explosion, and Zenrachi squeezed his eyes shut, aware this was the end.

When nothing happened, he opened my eyes again, seeing blue static flashing around his body as he was suddenly clear of the radius of her bombs.

"You can come out now, assuming you're not dead, that is," the Contessa's voice rang out.

"I just want to talk." From where he was crouched behind a tree out of sight, Zenrachi caught a glimpse of her haunting smile, right before he heard a sword slicing through the cold night air. The tree he was behind was cut neatly in two, and Zenrachi crept slowly out of hiding, emerging from the safety of the shadows. *If she wanted me dead, I would be already*, he thought.

"Are you this friendly with everybody?" he asked boldly. "Or is just me you're trying to completely erase?"

"Just those who don't belong in society. In case you didn't know, this is *my* land, and I'm not keen on newcomers."

"Can I at least have a name to go with such mystique?"

"You may not live long enough for it to matter," she replied, circling him slowly, like a tiger about to pounce on its prey. "Or maybe you will. I'll say this for you, you can hold your own for a lone wanderer. Some might even consider you a skilled warrior…"

"I'm no fighter," Zenrachi snapped. "Not anymore."

The Contessa gave a devilish grin. "Hmm… we'll see about that." As Zenrachi glanced around, searching for a means of escape, the Contessa continued to circle him. "You're free to run if you really want, but hear me out first: I'm here with an offer you can't possibly refuse. It's no secret, what's become of this land since the coup. And so my 'associates' and I have formed an organization whose purpose is to maintain the balance of this land. The Tsurasu have been collecting the ancient relics of the land of storms, slowly uncovering the mystery that lies behind the deities of old. Our leader has selected you to join us."

Zenrachi paused for a moment, a whirlwind of thoughts racing through his mind. "But… how in the world did you find me here?"

"All you need know is that The Contessa is good at what she does."

"I've been constantly on the move, keeping my head down," Zenrachi persisted. "Why go out of your way to find a ghost for your organization? Which, by the way, you seem pretty confident I'm just going to accept."

"Why yes, I think you'll be *very* interested in working to exact your justice," the Contessa purred. "The same justice that, I might add, was not given to Seijin, your beloved brother."

Her words angered Zenrachi, but as much as he wanted to fight them off, he also knew a part of him had waited long for such a chance. If this Contessa spoke with any truth to her words, his possibilities could be endless – even if that meant the very land he once called home must fall. He could fill his void in his heart, in his soul, through the organization she spoke of – through the Tsurasu.

It all sounded too good to be true. But in that moment, Zenrachi realized that the Contessa was right. He couldn't refuse. He would leave his life of constant wandering and desolation for a new one, moving forward through the dark clouds concealing his path. Where the gods had failed, he would finally act.

"… I'm in," Zenrachi spoke into the silence.

The Contessa smiled. "Excellent. Oh… just one condition, dear."

"And what is that?" Zenrachi asked uneasily, still unsure of her intentions.

"*Survive*… and our justice will soon be realized." She stepped toward him, and Zenrachi saw that he would need to defend himself once again. He rushed to attack first, hoping his sudden aggression would leave her off balance, but once glance of her eyes left him suddenly motionless, and she sent him sprawling to the ground with a vicious kick.

The newly awakened power of Horiau had taken a significant toll on Zenrachi's endurance, and he could feel his demise approaching. His bloodied hands dug into the dirt as he rose up with a final spurt of energy, the last he had left to give, rushing the proud Contessa. Shifting his shoulders, he heaved a punch.

In response, she held her open hands together to form a green orb, launching it toward him. He vanished from sight as the orb exploded and he reappeared behind her in a flash, driving a kick into her ribs and following this with an uppercut that sent her body into the air.

Exhausted, Zenrachi finally had no choice now but to let down his guard, and as the Contessa continued hovering in the air, she catapulted herself back into his direction, landing a ferocious kick to Zenrachi's chest. Infuriated, spitting blood from her mouth from Zenrachi's earlier attack, she spun back into the air and held her hands above her head. Several green orbs formed, floating above the ground around her.

"SHOW CONTESSA YOUR TRUE DETERMINATION FOR JUSTICE! OR DIE IN YOUR MISERY!" Her shout echoed around him – and then he could see only the cluster of green orbs racing toward him, and hear only her hysterical laugh as he faded out of consciousness.

"Well, she seems... nice." said Rahku from where he was seated on the ground, listening to the end of Zenrachi's tale.

"And that was just the beginning of our… odd alliance."

"So why is she hell-bent on killing you again?" Hisashi asked.

"I… may have left her in a burning tower after betraying her and killing Yogen – or so I thought," Zenrachi admitted.

Rahku shook his head tiredly. "Ah. It's all starting to make sense now."

Sins of the Forsaken

"The time had flown," Zenrachi continued in his tale. "Before I knew it, four years had passed with the Contessa. We were so different, yet at the same time so much alike. During sleepless nights I gazed at the moon and pondered. How did she deal with the void identical to mine? Where would the Contessa's path lead her, and should I also allow my vengeance to consume me like it was consuming her?

We spent much time away from cities and civilization after leaving Akibara. Tsurasu was an organization, but also operated like a group of shinobi given the right circumstances… and the right price. I returned to the small village that had become something of the home I needed. Secluded and alone, I was up most nights and slept while the sun was out. At the first sign of the sun appearing on the horizon, I would lay down and close my eyes.

It was one such dawn when the Contessa appeared again."

Zenrachi yelled, shaken from a deep sleep, eyes snapping open to see the Contessa standing over him. He sat up and rubbed his eyes. "What are you doing here?" he asked, still groggy.

"You know, you snore quite loudly," she replied. Arms folded, she leaned against the wall next to the bed. "We've been hired to kill a disciple."

"A what?"

"Someone proclaiming themselves to be 'the disciple' is going around killing people, terrorizing villages. And performing rituals by encasing his victims in some type of substance in an effort to please the song bird god, Kotori. Declaring his sacrifices will resurrect the ancient beast."

"Why would human sacrifices be to a *songbird's* liking?" Zenrachi raised an eyebrow.

The Contessa shrugged carelessly. "Doesn't matter to me – we've been paid in advance." She pulled out a thick wad of cash, grinning. "Anyway, to resurrect the song bird, you'd need a certain ancient flute whose echoing sounds are said to be not of this world. Its origin, as well as its creator, is unknown. And on top of that, you'd also need the stone that fits into the flute, and know the song to play, to resurrect Kotori. However, the stone itself does still exist. Yogen thinks this 'disciple' may know something of its whereabouts."

"So maybe you shouldn't throw bombs at him as soon as we identify him," Zenrachi pointed out sarcastically.

"And maybe *you* shouldn't leave the door unlocked when you sleep."

"… But it *was* locked."

The Contessa only shrugged again. "Then get a better lock. Yours is broken now. And be outside in five minutes. Where this disciple was last seen isn't too far from here. Hurry up."

"Sure, just come into my house making demands," Zenrachi muttered, hastily pulling on his outer clothing and snatching his cloak from the hook by the door."

"You say something?" the Contessa asked, peeking her head back inside.

Zenrachi was wise enough not to reply.

After some time traveling, the pair arrived at a village in search of their objective and paused, coming across a bloody and white mixed substance that made a trail leading across a bridge.

"Well, I think I know where to go…" Zenrachi was repulsed by the slimy substance, although the Contessa did not appear in the least fazed.

Following the trail, it led to a rocky cliff overlooking the ocean, where they discovered a man drawing odd illustrations onto the rock ground with a white substance. Behind him lay a corpse, still bloody. The gleam of his bald head shone as his eyes darted up, noticing the intruders.

"Welcome. You picked a good time to be an offering to Lord Kotori. I am the Disciple Hadeshi. I was just preparing my ritual. Will you join me for a prayer? It'll only take a moment."

"Your... ritual?" the Contessa inquired, coolly curious.

Hadeshi clapped his palms together and a strange ooze emerged from his parting hands. Raising them into the air, sludge shot out until a colossal wall surrounded them. As Hadeshi clenched and opened his right hand, a flame emerged above it, while in the next instant, several sharp spikes shot out of his left hand, each with a flame on top of each.

The Contessa glanced at Zenrachi. "As a martial artist, you've crossed paths with many fighters. Does one bearing some type of wax ring a bell?"

"No... no, this is very different."

"No matter," the Contessa said lightly. "Anyone blocking our path will be erased." She aimed one open hand at the strange man, forming an explosive orb. In response, an immediate shot of wax hit her hand, and it fell abruptly back to her side as the wax became rock solid.

Hadeshi gave a deep sigh. "Very well, if you're in such a hurry to die, then let us begin."

"Aghh, dammit, it burns like hell," the Contessa exclaimed, scowling in pain. Zenrachi dashed forward toward Hadeshi. He drove his fist deep into Hadeshi's gut, which quickly becoming stuck in a pool of wax. His hand began burning almost immediately as he pulled away, still stuck in a fist. The disciple slapped his hands onto the ground and a wall of wax rose up in front of him and the Contessa.

"Above you!" she shouted, awaiting the disciple's attack. But a hand burst suddenly through the wax wall, gripping tightly at Zenrachi's neck. He was pulled through the wall, struggling to free himself, only to be faced by a flame in the disciple's other hand as they faced one another.

"In the name of Kotori, those who do not believe… shall burn."

A sudden gust of wind sliced cleanly through Hadeshi's arm, sending it flying into the air. The flame in its hand dispersed as the lifeless limb fell to the ground. The Contessa raised the tip of her sword to the air, pointing it at Hadeshi, and drove her fist into the ground, breaking the wax that encased the other hand.

"AHH, YES! You two shall make a very pleasing offer to the deity of melody." Hadeshi screamed in excitement, wiping blood from his mouth. With one swift movement of the hand still attached to his body, the severed fist came flying at Allura. Her sword was knocked from her hand, and Hadeshi's arm melded back onto his body as the wax slowly reattached and hardened.

Not waiting to see more, Allura heaved a bombardment of green orbs at him. They exploded on impact, forming a smokescreen around him. When the smoke cleared, she and Zenrachi could both see the hardened wax shield that had formed over the disciple's head, protecting him from so much as a scratch from the Contessa's attack. Hadeshi began laughing as the other two hastily retreated.

"Dammit… any ideas?" Zenrachi asked the Contessa, catching his breath.

"Constant movement," she advised. "His wax allows him to attack or defend but has a delay to set up. He's practically a candle, his body will just form again when we hurt him. We need one big hit so he can't harden himself again."

"So, big explosions then – right up your alley," Zenrachi replied.

The Contessa gave a terrifying grin. "About time we did things my way."

Just then, the disciple heaved a punch that detached his arm again, send it speeding toward Allura. She created a huge orb to break the impact, but even so the punch knocked her off her feet, making her drop her sword again.

"Dammit, take the sword, I have an idea," Allura shouted, rising to her feet. The severed arm had fallen to the ground after clashing with her, and more wax was now quickly growing out of it. The wax soon formed a body, and a double of Hadeshi stood before them, a flame held in each of its palms. At the same time, the real Hadeshi's arms began dripping before they turned into wax blades hanging at his side.

"His abilities have been split between the two. You take the fire one, I'll take the real one," Contessa barked out to Zenrachi.

Zenrachi engaged the fire half of the disciple, swiveling from punches that sent bursts of flames brushing against his face. Hadeshi gestured, and the fire rose above Zenrachi until it stretched up all the way from his feet. A heavy, flame-shrouded kick swung across Zenrachi's face as he dodged wildly. He could see the stream of flames flow by as he tightened his grip on the sword in his hand, taking a heavy swipe upward.

Hadeshi's body was severed in half by the blow. The corpse slowly burned away, leaving only the original. From behind him, Zenrachi heard a myriad of explosions as Allura battled on. They fought tooth and nail, bright light flashing erratically and debris flying everywhere, forcing Zenrachi to shield his eyes.

He saw Allura summon a double of her own, which grabbed hold of Hadeshi. "Cut through them both!" she shouted as she leaped away.

Zenrachi aimed the point of his sword at Hadeshi, but his vision suddenly became doubled and blurry. His arm began to tremble as he struggled to escape the illusion, just as a sharp pain surged through his arm. In the distance, he glimpsed a shadowy figure that grew larger as it wandered toward him, speaking something in a low voice. Faintly, as though from far away. Zenrachi heard the Contessa yelling, trying to snap him out of the trance.

A silent flash of lightning blinded him, and Zenrachi instinctively squeezed his eyes shut. In the darkness, he saw two glowing red eyes. Distant yelling became louder until Zenrachi snapped his eyes open again to see Hadeshi break free from Allura's double. It became consumed in the wax left by Hadeshi until her struggles subsided. Then he sliced, dismembering it.

"Zenrachi, dear, do me a favor and GET YOUR SHIT TOGETHER. I can't summon another one. So now *you* grab hold of him and I'll do the rest."

Hadeshi slammed his hands into the ground and rose up again, grabbing his forearm and yanking it forcefully from his body. The arm rose into the air to form a long sword of wax, hard as any sword made from steel.

Zenrachi pounced. They clashed at lightning speed, trading several blows that sounded like crashes, flickering in and out of sight as they desperately fought.

"What the hell are you doing?" Zenrachi yelled at the Contessa, knowing he could not keep up at that speed for long. Out of the corner of his eye, he saw a glowing light of brilliant green. Allura leaped into the air, clenching her hand as she created a massive green orb, aiming straight for them.

"YOU CANNOT KILL ME... I WILL FOREVER TO SERVE MY DEITY," Hadeshi screamed out, his blade struggling against Zenrachi's.

"Tell your deity..." the Contessa said, now hovering for an instant in the air above them. "... *Bow to the Contessa.*"

The blast was large enough to send Zenrachi flying backward as Hadeshi disintegrated into nothing within the green orb. The power of the storm bird within Zenrachi saved him, flickering him away from the explosion. Even so, he was knocked back against the wax wall left by Hadeshi as he reappeared.

Looking at the massive blast caused a strange feeling to emerge from deep within him. Seeing friends and family die… he was used to this now, and he'd fought countless opponents over the years, yet never truly contemplated taking anyone else's life in the heat of battle. No matter whether he won or lost, he had always simply bowed to his opponent in respect and continued on to perfect his skill, his passion. Now his skill, the fire that burned within him, was slowly returning.

He would need to be careful not to use the mighty power of the storm bird in front of Allura, who he knew would stop at nothing to destroy any trace of Horiau.

"There's… not even a corpse left," Zenrachi spoke once the echoes from the explosion and the smoke had finally all cleared.

"Good, there shouldn't be," the Contessa said, tossing her head.

"Nice technique." He held up his hand to her.

"You should have been fine, he cut his own power in half when he created his double. But a strange technique he had indeed – I've never seen anything quite like it." She brushed away his hand, looking at it in confusion. "What are you doing?"

Zenrachi sighed. "Never mind- hey, wait a minute, you nearly killed me just now!" he shouted, suddenly remembering.

"You're still here, aren't you?" Her voice was nonchalant. "If you hadn't spaced out like that then you wouldn't have needed to dodge for your life."

"I'm not some pawn of yours, to go up in your blasts too," Zenrachi pointed out, scowling. "We're partners."

The Contessa's eyes grew brighter, and she spoke quietly but intently. "I suggest you be very careful with the next thing that comes out of your mouth. If you become dead weight... *you will be my puppet in an instant.*" She stared at him menacingly, and Zenrachi looked away. "We clear, dear?"

"… Crystal," he murmured, holding back his frustration.

"Good." The Contessa dismissed the topic with a flick of her hand, delivering her parting words. "I'll be over in Akibara at the Black Mamba later. Come have a drink – as long as you can handle something strong." With that, she shot a hole into the melting wax surrounding them, making her exit.

"I don't know if that was an order… or an invitation," Zenrachi said to himself. "And I'm not sure if I even want to find out."

Tournament of the Lotus

A few hours had passed by the time Zenrachi found himself looking up at the gold lettering outside the Black Mamba bar. He found the music intriguing, an entirely new sound to his ears, and it drew him inside where the soothing tunes brought him to a stop. Atop a stage, a woman sang in a language whose words Zenrachi did not recognize, although he could feel the various emotions in the words as easily as if they had been his own. Anger, pain, sorrow... the woman's voice echoed over the accompanying melody of a flute. Was it that the melody itself was merely pleasant, he wondered, or did the woman's sorrowful words mirror the melody of his heart?

A large crowd was gathered, and Zenrachi continued past them, making his way to the back of the room to see if Allura's summons proved true. He spotted her fiery red hair and several empty stools around her as he approached the bar.

"Well well, look who's appeared out of hiding. Ekora, bring me another round of your finest. I have a guest." She raised her hand, a cigar held casually between her fingers.

"Your tab," Ekora replied over the sound of the music. "I have the one you like." Two glasses abruptly hit the table in front of them. "And one for you, silver. She's usually more threatening than this – I think you might actually make it. Long as you can handle my special mix, that is."

"Can't be as bad as her nearly killing me in the crossfire," Zenrachi muttered.

"Oh, you have no idea yet how Allura can be, silver. She can get just *a bit* out of hand with her competitiveness, no matter what it's about."

The Contessa smirked, but did not reply. "Oh, here, I nearly forgot." She handed Zenrachi an envelope, a wad of money inside."

"Between all the explosions, I guess it must've slipped your mind." His reply was sarcastic, but the Contessa merely glared at him and downed her drink. Zenrachi followed suit, throwing back the light green elixir until the glass stood empty, staring back.

"Ekora, two more, dear," the Contessa declared.

"Add two more after that," Zenrachi cut in boldly.

Ekora's eyes widened. "This isn't going to end well," she said to herself, preparing more of the strange colored drink over which the pair seemed to be competing.

The two downed glass after glass. "Done!" they both shouted, stacking their glass on top of the several around them. The bar had gradually cleared out around them until only a few stragglers were left.

"Last call. Close up, guys, it's almost three," Ekora shouted out to the security at the door. She released the restraints from her hair, letting it down and sighing in a mixture of relief and exhaustion as her workday came to an end.

Allura was slumped over the bar, her head facedown, to all appearances passed out. "What do we do with… her?" Zenrachi asked, pointing and slurring his words.

"When she gets like this I bring her home with me. I stay at the inn right next door to the Black Mamba. Alright… you can come along too," she grinned, eyeing a drunk Zenrachi.

"Thanks, but I didn't ask-"

"Come on. You need rest, Bofu is far from here. In exchange, you're carrying her."

"But… I don't… oh, fine." He tried to pull Allura from the bar, only to have her slip from his hold a moment later, her body falling lifelessly to the ground. "I'm dead," he whispered in despair. But only a loud snore could be heard from the slumbering Allura.

"Just grab her, she won't wake," Ekora told him.

Zenrachi held the Contessa over his shoulder as he followed Ekora out a backdoor that led outside. It faced another door across a small alley into a building, where Ekora swiped a black card into the slit before a loud click heralded the door's opening. They walked up two flights of stairs opening a door revealed a whole hallway more of them. As Zenrachi stumbled along, his balance precarious, Ekora finally made a stop, sliding her card into a slot that read '1219' above it.

He followed her into a dimly lit room with a bed and couch facing a balcony as Ekora disappeared into another room. After setting Allura down gently on the bed, Ekora reappeared, standing in the middle of the hallway now clad in a diaphanous gown.

"You know, there's room in here for both of us-"

"I'll just crash on the couch," Zenrachi said, oblivious to Ekora's message. "I'll be out by the morning, I just need to sleep," he continued.

"Silver, I think you misunderstand. Come in here and-" Her words came to a sudden stop as both Zenrachi and Allura's snoring interrupted her words. She gave up, stomping back to her room and slamming the door.

Zenrachi awoke in the early morning, dazed at the gleam of the orange sun piercing through the glass. He wiped his eyes and sat upright on the couch, noticing the balcony door sitting slightly open. Grabbing his jacket, Zenrachi tied it around himself as he left the house, making it down the stairs and reaching the side door to ground level without meeting another soul. With one hand he held onto the wall, with the other his head, which was throbbing in pain thanks to the previous night's excesses.

He looked up as a familiar odor caught his nose. The alley between the two doors opened his view to the vast, lively city. He took a long look around before spotting the Contessa, leaning against the building and smoking her cigar.

"I was beginning to think I was going to have to come rescue you from Ekora's clutches." She exhaled a cloud of smoke before handing the cigar to Zenrachi. "I still have things to take care of here before I return to Bofu. What Sakumo does on the Tsurasu's behalf has nothing to do with me. I do things best carried out behind closed doors."

"And moving in silence," he replied.

"Glad to know someone's learning." There was a pause as she blew out more smoke. "There's a fighting arena near the market district. See Ekora for a way in there. But only when you're up to the task. The best fighters in the area, both crooked and clean, will be there. You may run into some old friends… or even some other Tsurasu members. They fight mostly for money, but there are some… interesting items that turn up there from time to time. In our case, a prize for a future tournament that you're going to enter."

"No explosions this time?" he asked, one eyebrow raised.

"Even I know there's a time and place for everything. You should leave the planning to me sometime."

"Hmph. So. A tournament?"

"That's right. Peace may be gone between the four nations, but riches aren't. The scum of the world still come to throw money at warriors whose passion was made into a means of survival. Mortals have simply revealed their true nature, clamoring for violence. I joined the Tsurasu to be the very destruction they desire, right up until the point it turns on them. A divine goddess to judge these mortals; a goddess of destruction. And a warrior to serve justice to the land that was taken from her."

"Allura, I've told you, I'm not the great martial artist you think I once was…" Zenrachi warned her.

"I'm well aware, but I have an idea. And you don't have forever, so it would be in your best interest to start with some type of training in the upcoming months."

"I don't like that smirk on your face. What exactly do you have in mind?"

"A disguise, for a start. You'll need a different look if you're going to be in front of crowds. We wouldn't want people to suddenly remember the face of the young martial arts prodigy of Dentori's past. Let's see here, a comb for that long hair, maybe a dress, some mascara…"

"Don't even think about it," Zenrachi snapped.

"Oh, fine, we'll just make some 'light' changes before you enter. We'll meet again when the time comes."

Zenrachi paused, looking up at the faces of Rahku and Hisashi, who were still listening quietly, not interrupting his tale. "I spent the few months I had been given in training for the tournament. Before I had become involved with the Tsurasu, I was lost, struggling to find something, anything, to go on for. And ever since joining, the void, the darkness within me began to brighten. The power that had been slumbering inside for so long pounced on the chance to release the fury I'd been containing after leaving Dentori. Seeing the truths of the land made me realize I needed to return, as unstoppable a force as this land needed. Paired with the Contessa, my eyes were opened to what people like us were truly capable of, even as those in power tried to break us down, make us weaker, yearning for our misery. The god's power within me slowly became my own, and I began to be able to withstand more of the strain it had upon my mind and my body. I became stronger, darker... like the very storm-infested land around me. And so, as the time approached when I would enter the tournament, a feeling of excitement at the chance to fight again was creeping in. I returned to the Black Mamba to meet with Ekora and the Contessa."

"Back here, silver," Ekora shouted back at Zenrachi, standing in front of a storage room door.

Allura appeared, a grin on her face and, Zenrachi didn't doubt it for a moment, a bad intention in mind. "Hmm, so many possibilities." She grabbed a lock of Zenrachi's hair, emerald eyes gleaming dangerously.

"Don't get any ideas. Just change my hair color or something. And do you have anything other than your shade of purple?" he asked, looking at her clothing, batting her hand away.

"Hmph. Fine. I had the perfect thing picked out, too." She put her hands out to Zenrachi, altering his hair color using one of her special techniques.

"There, happy? Something a bit more traditional for fighting, with a pattern similar to the one on my cloaks."

"Wait, how about this?" Ekora said, rummaging through boxes strewn across the storage room. She emerged with a silver mask that resembled the face of the storm bird, nearly identical to the one that had once appeared before him in the flesh.

"Wh-where'd you find this?" Zenrachi asked nervously, seeing Allura's disgusted look.

Ekora shrugged. "A costume party or something. It's been there since I've been at the Black Mamba, what's the big deal?"

"It'll work, just put it on," Contessa snapped impatiently. "Now come on, there's a guy to see about your entry. You just behave yourself, *partner.*" She brushed past Zenrachi's shoulder as she left the storage area.

Zenrachi trailed behind her as they walked to the other side of the bar. The people seemed to have cleared a path as she approached, and a man at one of the tables turned his head, seeing the Contessa approach. His large, circular glasses slid down his nose as he grabbed the end of a cigar hanging out of his mouth.

"Big, bad Contessa – to what do I owe the pleasure? Did I piss off the wrong person?" He reached into the jacket he wore for a small black box.

"I have a fighter for the Storm Arena's upcoming Tournament of the Lotus."

"You don't say. He got a name?" the man asked curiously, pointing to the masked Zenrachi. He put the cigar to his mouth again.

"Silver," the Contessa said firmly.

"Well, I do owe you a favor, so I'll tell you what, *Red.*" He exhaled a cloud of smoke. "Have eagle eyes here find me in the Storm Arena in two days. I'll get you in there, all you have to do is fight. So, what's a demolitionist like you need an ancient flute like that for? Holding a recital?" He raised an eyebrow.

"Let's just say I like to keep myself busy. It's Tsurasu business – and none of yours."

"Well excuse me." The man chuckled darkly, letting out another smoky cloud. "Like I said, Silver, on the day of come find me. I'll take care of things on my side. Only the best for the Contessa." He bowed ironically.

"Always good to pay you a visit, Manuki." The Contessa reached into a pocket for a small stack of cash, placing it next to him.

Zenrachi entered the Storm Arena just as planned two days later. Darting his eyes back and forth, scoping out the area, he spotted a black fedora with a feather sticking out of it. Approaching the man still wearing his gold circular glasses, Zenrachi nodded his head as he walked toward Manuki.

"Right on time, Silver. Let's roll then." The two walked to a nearby table where two other men sat, registering fighters. "Oh, and one last thing, where are you from? You know, for the announcers."

Zenrachi paused for a moment as Manuki readied his pen to fill out the form. "Suzuma, Dentori."

"Hmm, the name sounds familiar… ah yes, there was a young martial artist out of that small village once. Real talented boy. Yyolin Enenki's kid." He took a puff of his cigar, deep in thought. "Seijin, I think his name was."

"What happened to him?" Zenrachi could not resist the question, wondering exactly what Manuki knew.

"Murdered in cold blood. The domino to the power struggle between Dentori and the other three nations you see now. Some just can't live with peace – all those people and their different 'beliefs' result only in chaos. I hate seeing young stars from around Arashi Tochi brought down by the mess people made before them." Manuki frowned. "Heard he had a baby brother too, a boy who Yyolin the Phantom Fist took under her wing." He glanced at Zenrachi, grinning, clearly making the connection. "There may be darkness around that soul, but the light shines brightest in the dark."

"An uphill climb against those in power."

"Well, you're still alive, so I'd say you somehow managed to stay away from Yyolin's bad side."

"See you when I win, Manuki." Zenrachi threw out his fist to him, and Manuki smiled, bumping his fist against Zenrachi's, before striding through the wide doors that led to the arena. It was time to begin.

Zenrachi stood among several other fighters awaiting their seeding. All were looking toward a large black screen atop the arena. The first two fighter's names appeared on the board, then the next pair, and the next. Zenrachi's heart began to race. He saw his name flicker several times before it finally settled. He exhaled large as the gate to the arena slid open.

A hand grabbed his shoulder. "I made sure you wouldn't be fighting in the first round. Good luck to you, Silver. And remember, *watch closely*."

Manuki left as the first two fighters came forward for their bout. Zenrachi paid close attention to their movements as they traded blows back and forth. One of the fighters, Ame, was keeping his distance from his opponent, and Zenrachi observed him carefully.

Their struggle came to an abrupt end as the other fighter crashed into the ground, knocked down from high above him.

"K.O winner: Ame Galdono," declared the announcer as the crowd roared its excitement. "A mystical bow staff, not much of a close-up type, only defending when in close quarters. Using a long hand weapon to keep away while he lines up his shots from afar, with several different elements in his arsenal. A beam of energy shoots out of the dragon's mouth at a slow rate, but with grave results. That beam left his opponent's body singed…"

Ame stood tall, landing back easily on the ground following his airborne attack. He held a curved staff at his side, a dragon's head sculpted at the top. As though aware he was being observed, he turned his head sharply, eyeing Zenrachi before walking from the arena, exiting the doors on the opposite side.

The large screen at the top of the arena began flickering names again, and Zenrachi's nerves settled as his finally appeared again.

"Round two, Silver vs. Vas!" the announcer boomed.

Zenrachi stepped forward, a scowl behind his mask. From the shadows in the corner, a man appeared before him. His head was shaved at the sides and his hands and feet were heavily taped in red at the knuckles. In his hands he held a gleaming blade. The crowd cheered on as the announcer continued.

"Round two of the Lotus Tournament. Once again, last one standing, dead or alive after the ten-minute time limit wins the match. Winner of the tournament receives the legendary, and *very expensive* Lotus of the Storm Arena. Proctor, your call."

The proctor stepped forward until he stood halfway between the two fighters. "Fighters ready… begin!"

Zenrachi stole a glance at the crowd as an emerald gleam caught his eye. A blonde-haired woman saw him looking and grinned, winking at him. She had changed her appearance, but

Zenrachi could have spotted that evil expression a mile away. The Contessa was watching, just as he knew she would be.

But he had been distracted, and in that moment, Vas drove his shoulder into Zenrachi's, sending him flying backward. Zenrachi skidded to a stop right at the ring's outline, and Vas pounced again as Zenrachi regained his footing. He pivoted to his side and sunk a return punch into Vas, baiting the aggressive fighter. Now circling one another, looking for an opening, Vas made several swipes of his blade, grazing Zenrachi's arm but neither managing to hit the other beyond a few shallow swipes.

Vas broke free of their struggle and used Zenrachi's body to propel himself into the air, forming his body into a ball which began to spin with immense force. Then he came crashing down as Zenrachi quickly braced himself against the impact. The blow swept him off his feet, and he rolled out of the way as Vas yelled, sinking his knife into the ground where Zenrachi's body had just been. Rising to his feet, Zenrachi stood square to the other fighter and began swaying his shoulder back and forth, waiting for his opening.

"Just like Mother taught me," he said to himself, and began flickering in and out of sight around Vas. Each time he flashed before him, he dealt a punishing blow in between several feints, remaining too unpredictable for Vas to do anything but defend. After several such blows, Vas rushed toward Zenrachi in a rage, swiping at Zenrachi's face and screaming in renewed anger as an orange flame emerged from his jagged blade. He held it, trembling with rage as a tall stream of fire emerged from it. Then he pounced, swinging the blazing blade wildly. Zenrachi flashed away, using the storm bird's power to displace his physical self.

"You won't get me twice," Vas muttered with a grin, swinging the great flame backward into him, predicting Zenrachi's reappearance.

Zenrachi clutched at his arm, seeing the bloody slash marks. "Dammit, he got me." Wincing in pain, he kept an eye on the clock at the top of the arena, his shoulder throbbing.

Vas grinned and once again condensed himself into a spinning ball. But instead of carrying out his attack as he had the first time, he used this ball as a diversion, quickly reverting back to normal from as he launched his jagged blade straight for Zenrachi as the other rushed toward him.

Vas' defenses were left open as he reverted back to his fighting stance. The kick Zenrachi dealt him hit his chin, and Vas was sent flying upward. The movement was interrupted by a vanishing and suddenly reappearing Zenrachi, who kicked him still higher, then again and again, kicking Vas' body back and forth in the air, and finally appearing as a silhouette right in front of the overhead lights. A dark cloud shrouded Zenrachi as his last kick drove into Vas' body. It crashed to the ground, leaving a cloud of dust as Zenrachi descended from his airborne strike.

"Time's up!" the proctor announced. A surge of static went through Zenrachi, leaving him hunched over in pain, tightly holding his arm, but only he was left standing once the dust had cleared. The crowd roared as the announcement came.

"K.O winner: Siilveeer! He will advance to the final round in the Blaze Arena."

The crowd chattered excitedly. "Did you really think he'd win?" a voice asked, sitting alongside the blonde-haired woman in the crowd.

"No, but then, he tends to surprise me when I least expect it. It sounds like he's even become a fan favorite," the Contessa grinned.

"Yeah, and somebody's just became that much richer."

"I'll be richer still after *your* fight," the Contessa smirked.

Zenrachi walked through the doors on to the next room, following a flight of stairs leading up. The room had seats on one side, a large door on the other. A small screen faced him as two sets of stairs on each side led to the arena. The stone square appeared smaller than the last.

"And now, the Final Lotus. Silver of Suzuma, Dentori vs. Katsunke of Fubuki. Last fighter standing will receive the ancient instrument linked to the myth of the legendary song bird, Kotori!"

Both fighters stepped forward into the square arena. As they entered, the outside of the square became engulfed in flames. Atop a pedestal facing them stood the proctor.

"Your time limit is five minutes. Last man standing is the winner. Fight begins on first move. Good luck to you both."

"Concede this match now." His opponent broke the tense silence as their bout was about to begin.

"Hope you have a good reason to piss me off," Zenrachi snarled. The request made him uneasy, and he clenched his fists tightly.

"This eye here can sense energy and identify its nature. An ability passed down from generations of my clan. You want to know what this eye is showing me right now? I can glimpse only a sliver of it, but godly energy is within you. Energy with a thunderous pressure, emitting like great waves." Zenrachi's eyes widened as he realized his secret had been compromised. "Quit now and this will remain your secret alone. If not… well, you can go on living your life. Can't be all bad, right, *Horiau*? I mean, some revere the storm bird, putting it on a pedestal as a symbol of peace and tranquility. However, there are others hell-bent on its demise should it ever return. Viewed as the symbol of destruction, the regulator for mortals." Zenrachi heart began to race, knowing there was only one choice left to him now.

Kill...

The Contessa would erase anyone and anything from existence that stood in her way of becoming the god she desired. If this was revealed to her, if the Contessa became aware of Zenrachi's true identity... Zenrachi knew he'd be running forever, that she would never stop chasing him until her vengeful hand dealt its final blow.

"I have no choice... this fight will be your last." Zenrachi's eyes sharpened, altering the very atmosphere around them as he channeled his power.

The two stared each other down, each trying to read the other. Then the other fighter heaved his arms toward Zenrachi. Streams of water rushed out of his fists like cannons, knocking Zenrachi off his feet. The reaction from the wall of fire surrounding them caused steam to billow through the air, the clouds thickening as powerful strikes bounced off one another.

Katsunke disappeared into the steam and rushed Zenrachi's blind side. Zenrachi turned, only to see a giant ball of water emerge from the fog. Punches landed like knives to his gut as the sudden barrage from his side knocked him away. He skidded along the ground, trying to regain his footing, leaving his back open to a viscous kick followed by another surge of water. Zenrachi struggled to his knees, looking around wildly, seeing the large puddle of water resulting from Katsunke's attacks.

Katsunke had now formed eight arms made of water that resembled tentacles, his hands weaving signs in the air. His arms snapped together and the eight tentacles above him grew. Zenrachi looked at his own hands still on the ground, half-submerged in the puddle of water. Then he looked deep within himself, tapping into some of the storm bird's power. Static electricity emerged from his hands, and even through the pain this caused him, Zenrachi quickly stood, regaining his footing.

The tentacles heaved a barrage of water balls at Zenrachi, who circled Katsunke, quickly darting away to avoid the blasts. He finally came to a stop as an immense mist surrounded him. Zenrachi closed his eyes, his inner senses scanning for movement as the mist became too thick to see through. Watery arms flew by his face, followed by several more, and Zenrachi's eyes opened to reveal an unearthly blue glow emitting from them. He kept count of the arms swinging for him, counting only six. His enemy's technique resembled an octopus, extending its arms to attack. Zenrachi snatched the last two tentacles that reached from him, shocking him with his static electricity.

Katsunke fell to his knees, hurt by Zenrachi's attack, and Zenrachi walked up to him slowly, planting his hands into the ground to shock him once again. As the lightning emerged from his hands, the tentacles of his opponent dug into the ground, launching Katsunke into the air. As Zenrachi looked up, he saw the extra ligaments dissolve into water.

Zenrachi weaved a hand sign before holding his hands together, still as stone.

"You won't get me twice. Your fate is sealed, storm bi-" The words were abruptly cut off by Zenrachi's devastating blow from behind, sinking into Katsunke's back. Electricity surged through Zenrachi's hands as he sunk them into Katsunke's body, electrocuting him. Zenrachi didn't let up as the shock grew more and more intense. Finally, he lifted his shaking body into the air over his head. Katsunke flew away toward the edge of the fire... too close. Katsunke's body was incinerated.

The static dispersed as a large gust of wind from a wave of the proctor's hand swept the mist away, revealing the arena again. Only one figure stood there.

"Time!" the proctor called. There was a long moment of silence as he viewed the blood-showered fighting stage covered in red-tinged water. Zenrachi stood, hunched over in fatigue, looking down at his blood-covered hands.

"K.O." the proctor announced. "Your winner is... Silver!"

A single faint clap could be heard from the small observer's stage on the opposite side the proctor.

Two large doors slid open, leading to a downward flight of stairs, two torches lighting up another door at its end. Zenrachi proceeded on to the dark stairway. His hand suddenly slammed against the wall as he tried to regain his balance. A shock of pain surged into his head, distorting his vision. His only light were the torches at the bottom of the stairs. As he walked, the torch flames turned pitch black. He heard an ominous cry echoing in the distance, its roar sending chills down his spine. His eyes darted around as he covered his ears from the deafening sound. The feeling of something approaching could not escape him, the presence growing closer before it suddenly vanished. The black flames reverted to their yellow blaze, becoming clearer as his vision returned. He shook his head, trying to compose himself before the final door opened to reveal the large crowd awaiting the winner of Zenrachi's match.

"Nice job, Silver." Manuki approached from a door on the opposite side.

"You're… here to present the prize?" Zenrachi asked.

"Not exactly," Manuki chuckled. He removed his dark shades and jacket.

A proctor approached them, grabbing Zenrachi's hand and raising it up high. "Winner of the Final Lotus… SIIILLVVVEEERRRR." The crowd applauded wildly, chanting his name. "And now," the proctor continued, "an encore just for you, the new champion versus the reigning champion: Silver against… SPECTRE!"

Next to him, Manuki grinned. "Don't worry, this fight will have a shortened time. Let's give them a show."

Even exhausted, Zenrachi could not resist the challenge. "Give me all you've got then," he smirked back, shifting into his fighting stance as a jolt of fresh adrenaline began rushing through him.

Without further need for words, they dashed toward each other, exchanging blows at blazing speed. They pivoted and swung like choreographed dancers, each giving and receiving punishing blows as they fought at close range. The crowd shouted their approval as their display of combat resembled art in motion. Zenrachi concealed his storm bird powers, using them only to flicker in and out of sight around Manuki. He quickly appeared behind him, swinging his leg into the air and missing as Manuki suddenly disappeared Out of the corner of his eye he saw Manuki reappear from behind, and the following punch knocked Zenrachi to the ground, the crowd continuing to chant and roar in excitement.

"You're going to have to be quicker than that to beat me," Manuki grinned. He approached Zenrachi, offering a hand to help him up. "But I'll admit, not bad, kid. I haven't felt that much excitement in a while," he continued as Zenrachi took his hand. They both held their hands high to the thunderous applause from the crowd, impressed with the pair's performance.

Zenrachi lifted his mask as a man approached, holding in his hand's the tournament prize. "Your partner's through that door," he gestured, and handed him the legendary flute.

"Until we meet again… Zenrachi." He and Manuki parted ways as Zenrachi nodded in acknowledgement and made his exit, to a standing ovation from the crowd.

"Have fun, dear?" a voice called out as he walked through the door, the gray skies of the city of Akibara looming once more above him. Zenrachi saw the Contessa waiting for him, standing away from the crowd, counting bills in her hand. "Quite the show you put on. And… here you go. Your well-deserved winnings." She handed him a large stack of cash. "Along with your share of the winnings from the bookie."

"Wait, you… bet on me?"

"Hardly a bet. What better opportunity for a big payout? A late entrant concealing his appearance with a mask, and whose strengths and weaknesses are unknown to all except one in the crowd? Not to mention that *killer* mentality. Didn't think you had it in you, but you certainly showed otherwise with that performance. And while everyone fell head over heels for the masked fighter, I bet on Manuki as well, including your fight with him. A win-win if you ask me. Oh, and…" Contessa pulled out a flute identical to one just given to Zenrachi as a prize.

"How did you-"

"You want to know what I noticed while you fought here?" she asked, her gaze sharpening.

Zenrachi inhaled deeply, his heart nearly beating out of his chest. "Wh-what?'

"During your matches, Manuki brought me with him to present the prize. We got separated by security. Since I couldn't advance, I had to find another way through without making a scene. I found my way to a corridor lined with large vases. The tiled floor was booby trapped – stepping on certain tiles would have tipped the platform under the vases. As I carefully stepped, one of the vases tipped over behind me. I managed to catch it right before it hit the ground. When I looked inside it, I saw the numerous explosives within. If even one of those vases had fallen, I was history. And so, after some careful maneuvering-"

"You know how to be *careful?*" Zenrachi cut in.

"I had to make sure none of the vases fell so I wouldn't go up with the place." the Contessa frowned him into silence. "Even I wouldn't have escaped such a large explosion. After some swift maneuvering and extra set of hands from my double, I finally made my way across the booby-trapped room, got my hands on the display and switched them."

"But why go to the trouble of switching them?" Zenrachi asked, not understanding.

"Leverage, my dear… maybe someday, if you live long enough, it'll all make sense to you. The lore behind the legend, the piece needed to resurrect an ancient god from long ago. Such power will become desire; someone will surely come after us for this flute. But inside it, I discovered a secret message. I tried playing the flute, but it played a sour note and sounded congested. I slid the flute open, revealing a rolled-up piece of paper within its barrel. See for yourself." She unraveled the paper and handed it to him.

"These aren't words," Zenrachi noted immediately. "It's-"

"Sheet music," the Contessa confirmed.

"So the flute itself doesn't hold the ancient power of Kotori?" he asked, puzzled again at her intentions.

"Look, these deities have been gone a long time, and there's no need for them to return to existence now only to see the destruction they allowed before. No one should have to suffer the things deities like that bring to the earth, or to suffer a fate like ours. Let people keep believing the flute is some key object to summoning an ancient deity. In the end, I have an ace up my sleeve... plus, we got a surprisingly big payout from our little venture. Try not to spend it all in one place," she smirked.

Zenrachi broke off from his tale as Rahku retrieved a canteen from his cloak.

"How much of that did you bring?" Hisashi asked him at his side, catching a whiff of the potent brew.

"Just enough to get through this story," Rahku said, chuckling. He gestured to Zenrachi. "Go on, Zen. What did you do with all that extra cash?"

"I'd never held so much money at one time," Zenrachi admitted. "Sadly, most of it went toward competing with Allura. We drank and ate mountains of food, especially after whenever we consumed those herbs of hers. There were only a few more times we were called on by the Tsurasu after that, but each time was seemingly more dangerous than the last. Not that we couldn't handle it, but signs of foul play became more and more prevalent. I knew she felt something was off just like I did, but she was determined – nothing could sway her, or stand against her desires.

"So what happened next?" Hisashi asked.

"I was on top of the roof one night, seated beneath the moon's gaze. I… needed some air, some space. I was deep in thought when I heard a banging on the front door."

Zenrachi hopped back into the house through the window he had left open. By the time he got there, the Contessa had all but broken the door down.

"Ugh, what is it now. Wait, let me guess, another crazy cultist? Some new money scheme?

Whatever it is, it'll definitely involve blowing something up, I'm sure." She said nothing, only a fierce scowl on her face. "Wh-what is it?" Zenrachi asked, growing nervous.

"I've found the Storm Bird."

Zenrachi's heart beat loudly. "Wh- What do you mean?"

"We're going to Dentori. I've got a lead. There's a secluded jungle on the eastern coast of Dentori, separated from Bofu by a large waterfall. Get dressed – you should always be ready for battle. I could've been an assassin."

Zenrachi sighed and closed the door, emerging from the house once he had hastily dressed. They wasted no time in departing from Bofu toward their little-known destination, breaking the silence only to swap information about their mission.

"What can you tell me of this region we're entering?" the Contessa demanded. "It's your homeland."

"I never really went to the part we're headed for now; it's far out and not easy travel. It's also viewed as a sacred place, where the animals live freely from humans."

"Which means an unknown terrain in which to look for that damned bird. It must be there," the Contessa surmised.

"Well, where I lived, in the small village Suzuma, it rained often, leaving the soil rich with plants and tall trees. Not like the ones in Bofu where more structures have been built over time. There's less green the further west you go, with many more open fields than in Dentori. But down in the jungle, the animals are said to be king. A place sure to have secrets, and supposedly home to the bird of storms."

"Also said to be home of the dark storm that nearly wiped this land away," the Contessa replied bitterly. "Anything else, dear?"

"No, that's about it. Even if I knew more, I'm sure a nice surprise awaits us."

"Surprises are beginning to really irritate me." The Contessa clenched her fists.

"You and me both. But for the Storm Bird, we'll have to make an exception."

They reached the grass fields from the tropical jungle, as yet unknown to them. The Contessa came to a stop and removed her cloak, now wearing only her short-sleeved kimono. "It's far more humid here. I don't like *hot*. Besides, this land is strange... a land uninhabited by mortals." She gazed into the vast jungle, eyes fixed on a colorful bird flying out of a tree.

"By mortals, maybe, but there's plenty of life here. It is the animal kingdom that reigns supreme."

Hearing a loud chatter behind them, they were met by a group of small primates twined within the tropical trees. "What in the..." The Contessa stared, puzzled by the small animals that stood before them.

"They're... monkeys," Zenrachi said, slightly awed. "I haven't seen one in so long."

"Do these monkeys come with a death wish?" The Contessa's tone had shifted lower, her hand becoming engulfed in a familiar green aura.

"No, no," Zenrachi waved his hands, trying to stop her. "They're harmless, calm down." As his back was turned, one walked behind him, climbing up to his shoulder. "See, harmless," he said, petting it gently.

"The monkeys may have no issue with us, but not every animal is going take the idea of intruders so lightly," the Contessa noted. As she spoke, the monkeys began retreating.

Zenrachi looked to the one still on his shoulder as it let out a soft whimper. "Wait, why'd they leave?"

"Hmm. I don't know, probably because of those *strangely large* cats looking in our direction."

"Large... cats?" He looked over in the direction she pointed toward. "Oh... yeah, those aren't cats. And we need to hide, right now. Look, the tall grass over here."

"Hide? I hide from no one, and I'm certainly not going to start with an oversized feline," she retorted, sniffing.

"Dammit will you just come on." Zenrachi grabbed her arm, carefully moving into the tall grass.

"Get your hands-"

"Shhh! You can't just fight head on with everything you run into. Only more will come, alpha animals like that move in groups. Let's just hope they lose interest and leave."

Two lions approached the place where they hid as one stood atop a tree stump to survey the area.

"Um, dear-"

"But lions don't eat monkeys, do they?" Zenrachi asked himself, oblivious to Allura's words.

"*Zenrachi*," she hissed in a whispered shout.

"What?"

"What's that bulge moving under your cloak?"

"What are you- ah! Get off me!"

"It's that damn monkey."

"AGH! This little guy's grip is insane…" Zenrachi winced in pain, clawing to get it off his back.

"Shh! They're here." The Contessa crouched down low, concealing herself among the grass, and Zenrachi stayed still as stone as two lions brushed by the tall grass. Both humans held their breath as the two animals eventually lost interest and crept away.

"That could've gone really bad," Zenrachi whispered, finally getting ahold of the small monkey clutched to his back. As he held the small, startled animal in the air, a large shadow cast itself over them. "Now what to do with you-" His words came to an abrupt stop, and a third lion pounced on an unsuspecting Contessa, dragging her far out of the grass. She held her sword to its neck as sharp claws laid themselves right over hers in return. They locked eyes with the other, and Zenrachi gasped, sure he was about to see a huge amount of bloodshed.

"ENOUGH!" a distant voice shouted.

To Zenrachi's shock, the lion obeyed, releasing its hold on the Contessa and allowing her to get up. The jungle cat snarled at her. She growled back.

"Hello! I'm sorry, they're not fond of anyone in their territory – your scent probably made them wild. I'm Kagulo, are you two okay?"

"Yeah, I managed to get the monkey off my back," Zenrachi said, his heart still racing.

"Had a lot on your mind, huh?"

"No, I mean the actual monkey right there." He pointed to it, now wrapped around his leg.

"This little one is a little far from its family," Kagulo said, beckoning to it. He opened his hand, offering fruits that the monkey nibbled on as it hunched over his shoulder.

"Now, on to other matters. Why are you two here?" Kagulo directed his question to Zenrachi. "The people here aren't so fond of more humans entering this land, or even us either as of late. You don't appear to have malicious intent; however, Vadiga doesn't think the same of your partner."

"What significance does the storm bird Horiau hold?" the Contessa cut in, getting straight to the point.

"Ho… riau?" Kagulo was obviously puzzled by the name.

"Wait, the people here? I thought this land was uninhabited by mortals," Zenrachi interrupted.

"That's… partly true," Kagulo replied. "We have a small community that lives alongside the wildlife. About a year or two ago, the life in this jungle was nearly extinct. My pack was one the few signs of wildlife left in the jungle. Then, a sudden mysterious rainstorm came in from the west, and life gradually returned to the jungle again. The small civilization here grew. But with it came differences of opinions. I fear a war is on the horizon, and that my family and I stand directly in its path…"

"Your family?"

"Yes. I was found by a pack of lions who took me in as their own, and I stand to protect them now. There's no order between the people, and I'm too young and don't know anything about leading a civilization. But I am also no novice in hunting prey. The hunt, my pack, is what drives me. I am an outsider to the people trying to now overtake it. What they do not realize is that I know the whereabouts of the lost temple. Some trace of that… Ho-riau thing you spoke of may be found there. I hear the people speak of a pair of glowing stone that's linked to this part of the land as they plot our downfall. It's only a matter of time before things escalate. There are more hostile areas on the way there than there are here. Where we are now is on the outskirts of the small village. We'll have to go around and get there quietly to avoid wildlife."

"I will not be escorted by some child," the Contessa said, proud as ever. She began to walk, leaving Zenrachi and Kagulo to follow.

"What's her deal?" Kagulo whispered to Zenrachi.

Zenrachi gave a wry smile. "I'm still trying to figure that out for myself."

"Sunset is approaching. It'll be dangerous, but safer than going during daylight. We must move along the trees and tall grass. Remaining out in the open spells a death sentence. It's a diverse path, so stay close," Kagulo advised.

"If what you say is true, keep us alive then, boy," said the Contessa, not looking at Kagulo as she spoke.

"I will," Kagulo promised. "Alright then, what are your names?"

"I'm Zenrachi. That's the Contessa." They had reached the top of a hill, eyeing the area in front of them.

"We'll have to zigzag through this open area and avoid the predators here," the Contessa announced.

"What do you mean by predators?" Kagulo looked at her, nonplussed.

"Well, once upon a time I was a martial artist, and she's a very skilled fighter, so wildlife is a bit *new* to us." Zenrachi filled in for him.

"Well, for starters… there! Look." Kagulo pointed.

"Such strange spots," the Contessa noted, gazing from afar.

"That's a cheetah, the fastest of its kind."

"Hmm, a specialty in speed you say. Surely they cannot catch one such as-"

"Oh, they'll catch you without any trouble," Kagulo assured her, and the Contessa glanced over, not able to fully hide her shock. "They have extreme speed for hunting prey with those long legs of theirs, but they're not made for close combat or traversing up trees."

"What of that one over there. Are they working in tandem?" The Contessa's curiosity was piqued.

"Oh, that's not a cheetah. It's also a spotted cat and its legs are shorter, but they're much bigger in size and therefore stronger. lions are exceptional climbers, so trees like this provide no safety from them. We appear to be on the border of the radius of two different predators. Moving along the trees should keep us hidden, so long as they don't smell us."

"You can't talk to these particular cats?" the Contessa asked sarcastically.

"Only with my pack. Anything else will just see us as enemies in their territory." A moment after

Kagulo's words, they heard a loud roar as an animal, unseen until now, lay suddenly limp in one of the lion's immense jaws.

The three moved in closer, treading through the tall grass as the moon served as their only source of light. They weaved through the night jungle, eventually coming to another stop.

"Look, there is where my pack lives. Further down is the temple." They continued further downward, and on the edge of a patch of tall grass, Kagulo stopped them.

"That smell." Zenrachi recognized it immediately.

The Contessa nodded. "Blood. Fresh blood," she confirmed.

"We must go around," Kagulo concluded.

"Why? Those are the same kind of monkeys that greeted us earlier, aren't they?" Zenrachi asked.

"No... they're different. These monkeys are far more hostile when it comes to their territory. And they're not only fast, but also deadly at close range. And most of all... strength in numbers. If they get even a whiff of us, our position will be compromised, alerting every hungry animal within radius. We're gonna have to go around, keeping far to their left."

They continued on until Kagulo eventually broke the terse silence. "We're safe here," he said as two lions, half-hidden high in the trees, stared down at them as they approached.

"So this is your home?" Zenrachi walked alongside him into the lions' den.

"Yes, the pack that opened their arms to me and my-" A shadow suddenly descended from the tree nearest them, pouncing on Zenrachi from above. A small cloud of dust covered them. The Contessa readied a blast with her hand. When the dust cleared enough for the others to see, it was another person that stood atop him, teeth bared directly over Zenrachi's neck.

"My sister," Kagulo finished. "This is Litalia, the older of us two siblings. We both grew up along with the wildlife here."

"And I shall soon be the goddess of this jungle." Litalia let up, allowing Zenrachi to stand again. She stood taller than her younger sibling, thick locks of hair tumbling loose down her back, still eyeing Zenrachi like prey.

"From here is the end of the jungle's edge. You're on your own from here, I'm afraid," Kagulo said. "Remember what I showed you, and you'll be safe at least until you reach the temple. I have no clue what could be in there… or how the animals will react."

"Before you become mine," Litalia cut in, baring her teeth at Zenrachi.

Just then, a strange crackling noise could be heard from afar. All eyes darted up to see a fire, sending a trail of dark smoke into the sky.

"Oh no… it's happened." Litalia turned quickly toward her brother. "Kagulo! Go with Vadiga and the pack and confirm our suspicions. Remember, *do not engage.* No matter what." Dirt flew up as he obeyed, racing in the direction of the trouble along with his pack. Litalia, too, disappeared as quickly as she had arrived, leaving Zenrachi and the Contessa alone once more.

They progressed into the wild jungle in search of the ancient temple. In dead silence they moved through the small forest until the Contessa nudged Zenrachi, spotting a structure covered in moss.

"I think we've found our temple."

"Think the front door's open?" Zenrachi asked sarcastically, inspecting the temple. Thinking quickly, the Contessa shot several explosive orbs out of her hands and into the ground, launching herself up to the roof of the temple. Zenrachi climbed the stone wall, and through a large crack atop the roof they both made their way inside. The light was dim, and the Contessa used another explosive orb as a steady source of light as they explored the small temple.

"Allura, over here, look. Some kind of large container. And there's two of them." Zenrachi wiped the dust from them, revealing strange patterns all over it.

They both stepped back to look at them carefully. As the Contessa approached one, a tile sunk in as she stepped on the hard tile floor. Reacting quickly, she leaped into the air, seeing sharp spikes shoot out of the wall at her movements.

"What the-"

"I guess that explains how our buddy got here." Zenrachi pointed to the skeleton he now saw lying beside the casket.

Descending from the air, Allura carefully landed. Looking closely about her, she paused a long moment before finally speaking again. "This isn't a temple. This place... is a tomb. But for whom?" She held her chin, considering the possibilities. "I think it's time we saw what's really in these caskets. Lift that one, I'll lift the other," she ordered. The solid stone let out a loud rumble as they slid the caskets open. They side-eyed one another, wondering if they were both being greeted with the same sight from inside.

"This one wore a headpiece," the Contessa said. "Put to rest in fine clothing. The bone structure would suggest this was a woman."

"And I'm assuming this one's a man. But with bigger, denser bones than a person's. I also don't remember humans having large fangs like this." At his words, Allura walked over to see for herself. "Who were these people?"

"Likely once king and queen to these lands," the Contessa surmised. "Buried and honored by their people. Perhaps they did more than look and wave back in their time," she added sourly.

"Wait a minute! There's something else in here," Zenrachi said, rummaging through the tomb. He opened his hand to Allura, revealing the small yellow stone found inside.

She looked surprised, walking back to the casket she had opened. "Here too." She held an odd-colored stone in her hand, similar to its pair but paler. It lacked the faint glow of the one Zenrachi still held.

"You don't think these are-"

"Storm stones, unaccounted for because they were here the whole time? Maybe, but like those stones, they're useless now." From outside the temple they heard a low rumbling, reminding them of the chaos on the horizon. The Contessa narrowed her eyes. "I'm curious to see what chaos mortals have created this time. Hold on to these until we leave this jungle." She handed

Zenrachi the other stone, and they made their way back outside to the roof of the tomb, returning quickly to the trail in the jungle that led them there, now completely empty of wildlife.

Making their return to Kagulo and Litalia, they found all of the animals in a large group. Carefully weaving through them, Zenrachi saw Litalia sobbing and Kagulo approaching, a lion held in his arms. Zenrachi assisted him to lay the large cat down gently to the ground.

"We found these in the temple," Zenrachi said gruffly, holding back his tears but unsure how to openly show his pain. Kagulo took one, passing the other to his sister. In their grip, their hands stained with blood, the gems started to glow.

"Ahem," said the Contessa, gaining everybody's attention.

From afar, people were approaching, and Zenrachi could see from the sunlight flashing off the metal that they were armed with swords. Seeing the approaching mob, Kagulo and Litalia clenched the stones tight in their hands, anger and sorrow plain in their expressions. The stones gleamed brighter, and as the two snarled violently, the power grew and overflowed.

Allura backed up, forming a green explosive orb from her hands. "They're out of control," she shouted at Zenrachi. "They'll come for us before the villagers get here." Litalia leaped toward Allura, catching the orb shot at her and her own hand swinging it straight back at Allura. The Contessa took a direct hit, skidding back into the dirt. She rose to one knee slowly, wincing in pain.

A barrage of arrows from the approaching mob scared the animals into disarray. Zenrachi grabbed hold of Kagulo as his body transformed. His sudden strength overpowered Zenrachi's grip. Breaking free, he leaped above Zenrachi, sending a barrage of kicks to his face. Leaping back, the blows grazed Zenrachi's arm before an orb sent Kagulo flying away.

"The village people have come for their land. This isn't our battle; we must leave now," the Contessa said. "Their power is amazing – they're going to rip those mortals to shreds. Serves them right," she smirked. She rose to her feet, and Zenrachi quickly followed suit. They had to escape Kagulo and Litalia's outlash.

"What happened to him?" he asked.

"An overflow of power. He's too young to control it; a mix of jungle cat and warrior. All humans are his enemy now, he won't recognize us."

"And the other takes power and fires it back against his attacker," Zenrachi finished. Kagulo was as large as Zenrachi now, his fangs those a jungle cat and a similar pattern decorating his transformed body. "But… will they survive their own rage?"

Downpour

Zenrachi paused once more in his tale. "That was our last mission before we met one final time."

"You mean almost your last mission," Hisashi interrupted.

Zenrachi ignored him. "Tension grew between us and the Tsurasu. We had brushed up against the unknowns of Arashi Tochi, and with death, too often for it be simply coincidence. My next meeting with Allura would be my last. Our paths crossed once again as I sat down in a quiet tea shop."

"Good evening, can I get you anything?" A woman greeted him cheerfully, her tone familiar.

Zenrachi glanced down at the menu. "I'll have green tea with the soup."

"I'm afraid it's going to have to be to go, sir," the waitress replied.

"What- will you quit it!" Zenrachi yelled, seeing who his waitress really was. Then he sighed, rolling his eyes. "I can see I won't get to eat. Just tell me on the way."

"Not even a hello." The Contessa looked at him in disgust as they left the small shop, she tossing the uniform she wore in a passing dumpster. Beneath it was her usual kimono and cloak.

"And what excuse have you now for showing up like this?" Zenrachi asked, walking alongside.

The Contessa scoffed. "Not me. Yogen has summoned everyone to Envo Kahn Tower in the forests of Bofu. He said there's a message for each of the Tsurasu. Whether Yogen is there or not, he expects us to be there for his next order."

This may be my only chance, Zenrachi thought to himself. *This Yogen Allura speaks of... he must hold the true answers. What I've been searching for, all this time....*

On the way to the rendezvous with the rest of the Tsurasu, the pair came to a stop at the edge of the Bofu forest, looking out over a wide river

from which Dentori could be seen from afar –
the place Zenrachi had once called home.

There was a long moment of silence, with the
only the sound of the strong gusts of wind raking
through thc tension in the air.

"Do you see it?" Allura asked, looking in the
same direction. "The tournaments, the storm bird
your people speak of, your comrades… this is all
your past now, not your future. Have any of
them given an answer for the chaos? Has that
ancient storm bird descended from the lightning-
filled skies to stop such things from happening?"
She spoke softly, but her words struck hard.
"You've been forgotten by Dentori now… along
with any good you've brought them." Her voice
was chilling.

*Were such words more shocking to believe, or to hear from
someone other than myself?* Zenrachi asked himself
silently.

"To think it's been three years since we first
crossed paths and you're still alive," Allura
continued, oblivious to his thoughts.

"You mean the day you nearly killed me even after I agreed to join up with you?" Zenrachi scoffed. "Oh yes, tons of excitement!"

"You're still here because of me too," the Contessa reminded him. "You could have returned to Dentori whenever you wished – but I think you see the bigger picture in what we do."

"Hmm." Zenrachi was noncommittal, but the Contessa did not appear to hear him.

"And my ascension shall come... the storm clouds cannot protect you," she spoke aloud, seemingly to herself in a low voice. "I will be the one to cut. You. Down, Storm Bird."

Something sharp zipped through the air close to them, catching Zenrachi's attention as they walked through the gusty forests of Bofu. They stopped, Zenrachi looking around in search of the sound's source. His eyes spotted something moving from far away as an ominous glint lit the tip of bow and arrow.

Grabbing Allura, Zenrachi held her against a tree in the nick of time, sparing her life from the arrow flying toward them. He stumbled against a tree root, their bodies separated only by a breath as Zenrachi's heart raced. For the first time, he stared deep into the lethal eyes of the Contessa and for once, saw uncertainty there and surprise. Her hand held onto Zenrachi's face as she-

"Oh boy, here comes the good part!" exclaimed Hisashi, cutting into Zenrachi's story. Zenrachi glared at him.

"...Before she pushed my face aside as she surveyed the area, her eyes darting about for the arrow's origin," Zenrachi finished. "Now shut up, Hisashi."

"We need to move, we're sitting ducks here," the Contessa instructed calmly.

For once, Zenrachi was in complete agreement. Their only choice now was to run, for there was an archer high somewhere above them, cloaked in the trees and trying to ensure they didn't make it out of the forest alive.

An arrow grazed Zenrachi's face, barley missing his head as the Contessa grabbed his cloak, jerking him out of the way just in time.

"If we stop moving, we're as good as dead. This is no ordinary shooter. Don't fall behind!" she told him, running ahead.

After what felt like endless running, an ominous light exposed the forest's ending. Escaping the dense greenery, they ran out through a large patch of grass… and straight toward a cliff, where they found themselves cornered. A waterfall faced them, a bed of rocks at its bottom. Behind them, the forest archer had caught up, and another arrow whizzed through the air to land near their feet.

"I make it to be a seventy-thirty chance we survive a jump into the fall. I'm going to let off a blast to propel us away from the rocks. But how are they covering ground so quickly?" Allura said breathing heavily from running.

"Uh… that's a seventy for us surviving?" Zenrachi asked hopefully, letting out a nervous laugh.

The Contessa gave an answering grin. "You feeling lucky, Zenrachi?"

There was no time for more words. Allura held her hands together, murmuring in some strange language before a double appeared before them. Another projectile came whirring into the ground, this one creating an explosion behind them. The overhang they stood on began to rumble dangerously. Quickly, Allura weaved complicated signs in the air before hunching over, clearly fatigued. Her double dashed into the forest, creating a diversion. "She's going make a run for it. Hopefully our attacker will follow. I made it so she can withstand those hits. It's now or never for us! Brace yourself!" she yelled as the earth began to crumble beneath them.

This can't be the end… Seijin. First you, now I'm staring death in the face… please, Seijin, don't let it end here…

They both leaped down the waterfall, disappearing into it.

The light raindrops on Zenrachi's head awakened him, and he rose slowly to his feet in pain, wiping away the gray strands of hair masking his eyes.

"Where... am I?" he asked himself, glancing around at the lake surrounding him. His head was ringing, and he could hear ominous sounds in the air as though numerous voices were calling out to him. "Am I... dead?"

The voices grew louder, overlapping one another. He felt a presence lurking behind the trees out of the corner of his eye. The pain grew stronger, and Zenrachi looked down at his body. "Aghh! My arm. I-it's out of place." He clutched his limb, limping toward the gaze he felt from further among the trees and using them for support. The person hidden among them did not flinch at Zenrachi's approach.

"Allura!" It was evident at just a glance that she was severely wounded. His heart gave a jump as she turned away from him, revealing an arrow through the side of her head. One arm was completely missing from her body, mangled flesh hanging from her shoulder like it had been shot off.

She said nothing at all as she grabbed what was left of Zenrachi's cloak sleeve, leading him deeper into the misty forest.

How is she standing? What… is she? Zenrachi rubbed his head as the severely damaged Allura led him to a canal. Along the edge of it, surrounded by broken trees, lay his partner.

"Allura!"

He inched his way closer as the double strayed behind.

For once I can get a look of those eyes without the risk of falling under her control. Lost in thought, his mind racing as he debated his options, a familiar voice finally broke the silence.

"Are you going to help me or what?" The Contessa opened her eyes, looking at him unfazed. Zenrachi jumped, startled, and one-handed, began lifting the debris that covered her. His other arm was dislocated and unusable.

Dusting herself off from the debris, Allura extended her hand as her double approached her. It produced some kind of string from her mouth like a spider, and her double's cheeks expanded from the thin gray thread.

"Ugh." Zenrachi stared in disgust. Meanwhile, the Contessa, along with her double's help, used the thread to stitch up the several lacerations she had suffered from her fall.

"This same thread is what I once used to keep you alive," she snapped. "Who do you think bound your wounds back in Akibara?" She finished her task quickly before speaking again. "We must keep moving, battered as we are. There's no telling what lurks in the shadows of this forest." Her duplicate lost its physical form and became an aura, shrouding Allura within it. The dirt and scars disappeared as she was healed.

"Well, aren't you just full of surprises?"

"More than you could ever imagine," Allura said, taking a deep breath. She walked over to him until they stood face to face. "Stay still," she ordered, grabbing Zenrachi's damaged arm. "On three, I'm going to put your arm back in place, understand?"

"I don't have much of a choice, do I?"

"One…

A surge of pain ran through Zenrachi's shoulder as it made a soggy noise, shifting back into its socket. "Ahhh! Dammit…" He winced in pain, clenching his teeth. "You said on three."

The Contessa only shrugged. "We're in a hurry. Now quickly, there's no time to lose. Follow."

"There was a long silence as we walked through the forest until we were sure we weren't being followed," Zenrachi continued. Rahku and Hisashi were mercifully quiet as Zenrachi spoke of this part of his journey. "The silence was finally broken by some unexpected words."

"All of them… are dead because of their betrayal," the Contessa said suddenly. "They were afraid of the power, afraid of my creations, fearful of the storm that brewed within me."

Even by her standards, Allura was acting strangely. Her words sounded almost uneasy, and Zenrachi stared at her. "You… feeling okay?" he asked. When she did not answer, he stepped in front, confronting her. "We were the ones hunting people down, eliminating them from this world. Not the other way around. I'm sure you've killed enough people not to be rattled by someone trying to do the same." Zenrachi paused, thinking. "… Or maybe it's just that nobody's ever tried to save you."

The Contessa gazed up at him. "… Just consider us even." Her eyes sharpened, glowing a familiar green again, visibly rattled by his words. "Don't get your head shot off trying to be a hero. I should've known it was inevitable that we'd be targeted like this, but… my guard was down. Foul play. It's been going on even after the pact between nations."

"Wait, what are you saying?"

"As you well know, winning the combat tournaments brings funds to the victor as well as the nation they hail from. This eventually caused other nations to allow their greed to overcome them. I bet you heard tell of a 'sudden injury' with some of the entrants, when really they were removed to sway the results. Nations would even take their own entrants at times, wagering accordingly. Foul play at its finest. The only difference now is that everyone has picked definitive sides as the lines created by an uneasy peace have blurred over the years. Each nation, or groups like the Tsurasu, now pursue their own goals. Until the day it all reached breaking point When an all-out bloodbath broke out right in Dentori and-"

"Don't. Trust me I know," Zenrachi cut in before she could finish. "Its significance means nothing now."

"And now, it's all caused this major divide and a struggle for power – and it only has one outcome. Complete destruction." The Contessa looked at him, speaking plainly. "That's what we're here for, of course. To break the cycle of destruction, be the pillars of prosperity that the legends told of in old, dusty books could never foresee."

The Contessa's Last Dance

Evno Kahn Tower looked out over the once green pastures, now turned to dirt and rock. Here, Zenrachi and the Contessa found three other members of the Tsurasu as evening fell; Sakumo, Luarah and Midoro. There were no first introductions. It was dead silent, the tension clear in the air.

Sakumo gave Zenrachi no more than a brief glance, his eyes narrowed. Though nothing was ever said, Zenrachi knew that Sakumo considered him a rival, and was driven to outdo Zenrachi at every turn.

"Oh, have the great ones fallen?" asked a surprised Luarah. She was the heir of a prestigious ninja clan in Fubuki, and Zenrachi wondered what had caused someone who so proudly represented their clan to turn to such a group. *Although, no doubt she would say the same about me*, he thought to himself.

"So what's this about?" Zenrachi said to Midoro, intrigued by the sleeves of his overcoat waving lifelessly in the wind.

"Don't know, our business with the boss is done. I just wanted to see Dentori's phantom with my own eyes," Luarah answered, standing next to him.

The three went their own way as Zenrachi and the Contessa made their way inside the old tower.

"I found the scroll. It's a long, coded message." The Contessa was quiet, not wanting to draw attention to her discovery.

"What should I-"

"Go walk around or something," she said, waving her hand at him to shoo him away. "I need quiet to decipher this." She was already examining the scroll intently.

Zenrachi ventured through the tower, made up of several floors, looking at the trails of battle fought throughout time. Eventually, he came across a room with what appeared to be winged beasts engraved at the top of each corner of the ashen-stone wall. Below them were what looked like stones; three each below the song and storm birds of legend.

From what Zenrachi had learned while living in Dentori and after seeing the land of storm's secrets, the purpose of these deities were to keep peace over the land known now as Arashi Tochi. From his time with Allura, he also knew that parts of the truth and their sins had been swept away over the decades, with different stories being told among the nations as time eroded memory and stories were changed and embellished. Some stories told of a god of creation descending from the lightning-infested skies, while others told of a god of destruction descending from the sky, wreaking havoc with each flap of its mighty wings. Alongside that bird was another deity that sang a song of peace as it flew high, circling the land of storms.

"Or a song of death as destruction soon came after..." Zenrachi whispered to himself.

"And gaining such power through the gems would make for a powerful warrior," spoke an ominous voice from behind him, walking into the room. "But all of them? A boundless warrior. Mortals have no gratitude for their long time of peace. They are still stuck in their ways, still living with hatred. This will be a well overdue reform." The man appeared to study the walls in front of him and the stones below the engravings. "Isn't it glorious? Our purification of this world. Soon, it will be complete. You two did an excellent job obtaining that gem for me in Akibara. I hear you two even put on a stellar show."

"So why do you need those stones like the ones up there?" Zenrachi asked him.

"That was only the beginning." Yogen did not seem to hear him. "Soon, I will awaken the power in them, and offer it to the nations of Arashi Tochi in exchange for their survival."

"What?" Zenrachi recalled Allura's earlier words to him: *They're mere jewelry at this point, those beasts can't be revived.*

"These legendary birds went mad trying to keep peace between humanity. Mortals cannot live together in peace, understanding one another. Trusting them required the biggest *leap of faith*," Yogen said with a grin. "The coup was only the beginning, you know. "I don't have go out of my way to kill your loved ones for you to seek out power through me. No matter how kind hearted the being, life will always take. And take. And take. And eventually, all you're left to do is call out to the sky for an ancient deity to appear to take pity on you. On all of them. One will either disappear into an abyss of despair, or else find the god that lies within them and take over their world. Oh yes – life will always try to break you. No matter whether you're the head of a clan or a wandering shinobi, all it takes is that one bad day for your eyes to see the truth." Yogen looked at Zenrachi, his eyes drinking in the other's face. "Ahh yes, I see it in your eyes, your lust for something greater. Or maybe your time with the mighty Contessa has changed the both of you." He sighed. "Your pain is inevitable. Your suffering, however, is a choice. Soon, all the suffering shall be gone, when the might of the Storm Stones are under my rule. I will rule and there will only be peace! A new tournament shall bring both pain and prosperity to the land of storms. This Cycle of pain these mortals endure shall soon come to an end. The storm shall not be merely myth or a symbol of religions that mortals worship, using it as one of false hope. No, the gods will be resurrected to judge all those who inhabit their land of storms…"

Yogen's voice hardened on the last words, and Zenrachi struggled with himself, questioning. *Is Yogen right? I've spent the last several years serving as a force of regulation for the underworld of Arashi Tochi. For this? But I won't end up like Horiau did. I've spent most of my life trying to prove a curse, or predestined fate, dead wrong.* "Or die trying to be the hero." Allura's voice echoed in Zenrachi's head. *I'll spend the rest of my life proving it all wrong. I'll die before I stop fighting to let someone decide my fate 'fate' define me.* Another voice in his head whispered to him. The way things were is of the past. *Fighting is for the flame in your soul, not for survival. But Yogen and Allura's point whereas not so wrong. What better way for someone forgotten by their comrades to make a return as the very thing they've been told to fear all their life…*

Zenrachi stopped and looked about him – at Rahku, staring at him in shock, Hisashi with much the same expression on his face. "I had the power of the very deity of Dentori, and I was done serving an organization for another's gain," Zenrachi continued, remembering. "From then on I declared that I was indeed the god of my own universe. As well as the power of the storm deity. A part of me wanted to indeed be the balance to the land of storms… even if a part of me held malicious intent toward the very place I once called home…"

"Zen…" Rahku shook his head.

"And so, as Yogen's back was turned, looking at the wall, embracing the engravings upon it, I channeled my energy together with the storm bird's spirit. Electricity crackled around my hand, creating as deadly a sword as any that had ever been crafted. I plunged it right through his heart… or at least, I thought I had."

Yogen seized Zenrachi's arm, grinning at his failed attempt on the other man's life. "My my, what do we have here? The energy of the legendary storm bird. I'm honored, truly. Not only have you helped me in my mission, you've brought something far greater than any gem… one of the bird deities straight to me? Such a weapon you have here would certainly have killed me without this eye here to sense the power of a deity. Look familiar?"

"Katsunke… you stole his eye from his… remains. But how would you know… unless you sent him to the tournament for the Lotus Flute. 'The biggest leap of faith?'" He played Yogen's words back in his mind, seeing the truth of it now. Yogen had been behind everything. He'd sent in a member into the tournament, Ame, to win in case Zenrachi had failed to do so. He'd recovered that eye in an effort to find Horiau. The archer he and the Contessa had encountered in the forest had probably been Ame as well, forcing them to jump down the waterfall that looked to be their final resting place… and Yogen had known they would figure it out eventually; that, or that the Contessa would at some point rebel in order to achieve her own goals.

Yogen gave a sigh. "So I assume this is your... resignation from the Tsurasu. Well, I understand. I really do wish you all the best..." Still holding Zenrachi's arm firmly in his grip, Yogen cracked his wrist nearly in half, grinning as Zenrachi fell to his knees, screaming in pain.

But as the pain threatened to overcome him, an enormous roar left the tower rumbling as a surge of rage merged with the spirit of the storm bird inside him. The static energy surging through him made a thunderbolt in his clenched fist. Throwing it forcefully, it flew toward Yogen, piercing his heart... yet still Yogen appeared to feel no pain, although his body was damaged unto death.

The man let out an almost hysterical laugh. "You must strike the Voray stone twice before it sets, for the storm and the song will arise to a new fight, you fool!" Black smoke surrounded his corpse as it vanished. The thunderous roar, still continuing, caused the whole tower to start breaking down as the seconds ticked by, smoke and debris break away from the building.

Zenrachi was forced to find an escape, his energy depleted and both body and mind exhausted. At the end of the room, one corner of the tower had broken off entirely, revealing a crescent moon in the night sky. Zenrachi focused on this and ran, and ran… but the moon got no closer.

Suddenly he felt drops of rain on his head, pouring from the sky. All around him was pitch black darkness. Uneasy, Zenrachi took short, gasping breaths, the storm deity within him creating illusions before his eyes. Zenrachi wandered, lost, as rolls of thunder pealed and lightning flashed, impairing his vision. He stumbled through the storm, these flashes of light his only source of light. Stumbling over something on the ground, he wiped the mud from his face and looked closer. Another sudden flash of lightning revealed a body with a gaping wound.

"Seijin?" Zenrachi called out to it, holding his brother tightly as he fell to his knees, the rain pouring over him. In the next moment his eyes widened as he began to see cracks emerge over his brother's body. Looking up, he saw the world around him cracking like glass, the cracks deepening by the moment. A bolt of lightning came crashing down, shattering the body of his brother in his hands like glass. Zenrachi scrambled frantically for the pieces, trying to pick them up. The razor sharp fragments left his hands bloodied, and he let out a loud scream of rage and sorrow that echoed the storm bird's inside him.

His roar of agony shattered the illusion around him, returning him to the ancient tower that had begun to crumble. He rose to his feet, trying to compose himself from the dark illusion that had nearly consumed him. The ground rumbled as he ran, seeking an escape. He could now the see the moon now, getting closer through the corner of the tower. *Almost there!* His breath came heavy and gasping.

A bridge separated the two sides of the floor. Zenrachi dashed to the bridge when a green orb flew past his eyes, destroying his means of escape. The blast knocked him off his feet, and he hung precariously onto the bridge railing left by the explosion.

Now he could hear the clicking of heels walking closer to him, but in the darkness could only make out the etchings on the mask of Horiau he once wore alongside the eerie, green glow of a pair of eyes gazing in his direction.

"Leaving so soon…" the Contessa said angrily, emerging slowly from the shadows. Around her green irises, her eyes were bloodshot, and her hands, engulfed in a dark green aura, trembled with rage. "You have no idea what you've done. YOU DARE CROSS THE CONTESSA." She panted heavily, her furious scream echoing through him as Zenrachi hoisted himself to safety and scrambled back to his feet. "Do not worry," she continued when Zenrachi had no answer for her. "A change of plans won't stifle the Contessa. The only one now standing between me and my ascension, my vengeance, is no longer Yogen. My *sole* target… is YOU…

you and that bird," she hissed, unable to contain her terrible fury.

She knows… Zenrachi quickly realized the grave situation he was in, and fear threatened to overwhelm him. The Contessa stood in front of the broken bridge, forcing him to slowly back away.

"This will leave this tower in ashes, along with the storm bird… I was saving such an attack for a certain someone when the time was right, but this… this will now be *your* final act."

The tower would not hold up much longer, what was left of it ready to crumble at any moment.

"I'll tell you what. I'll give you a ten second head start so you can cling to what's left of your *pathetic* life for just a bit longer… *partner.*"

The explosive she had formed as she spoke was an echo of the deadly green glow of her eyes, and Zenrachi could already feel the air sizzle with it, burning.

"Ten… nine…"

He was staring death in the face once again, at the hand of the same person he had spent the last few years of his life with – not just as a partner, but as an ally who had the same dark cloud over their head, made up of grief and rage. The Contessa was not simply an ill-tempered vixen. She had something relentlessly driving her actions, was someone who possessed supreme fighting skills, and had a love for noodles and whiskey. Despite the constant death threats, wild plans and treacherous situations she exposed him to, Zenrachi had thought they were friends…

Divinity light, she called it. He could feel the intense heat radiating up chest, but knew that in his condition, running was pointless. Zenrachi was drained of power and could fight no more.

"Eight… seven…"

One of her hands gripped the railing of the bridge as she struggled to focus all of her energy into her other hand. She clenched her teeth hard, growling angrily under her breath.

"Six…"

The shaking grew stronger by the second as her angry scowl abruptly lightened. Now she looked at Zenrachi curiously as he stood in front of her, unmoving.

"Five… Four…"

The Contessa's arm began to shake from the pressure of the blast she still held. She looked almost afraid to release the massive explosion, which would surely erase Zenrachi completely from existence.

"Three... two... one..."

Ducking her arm extended toward him, Zenrachi quickly grabbed her, pulling himself close – close enough to steal a kiss, shocking her... and buying himself enough time to escape before she could recover. The last he saw of her was her eyes, wide in uncomprehending surprise, glittering as green as emeralds.

Zenrachi smiled slightly. "I thought it only fitting to outdo Allura by her own methods," he said to Rahku and Hisashi. That 'final act' of mine allowed me to escape with my life, if only barely. The echoes of Allura's screams haunted me as I made my getaway, her sheer outrage truly a thing of terror. I had a horrible feeling we'd cross paths again, and certainly not on good terms. The tower came crumbling down then, but up above, Allura's blasts shone gracefully in the night sky, arching up like fireworks before my eyes."

"Zen..."

"I couldn't help but gaze at them in awe, remembering the good times I'd had with her since Seijin… since the hole in my heart appeared. Allura understood me, she had seen the truth of life, and my experiences with her had altered me forever. Yogen, too, was still alive and out there somewhere, and I knew he wouldn't stop until the world became one of peace, achieved through fear."

Sitting close to one another in front of the fire to keep them warm from the snowy winds of Fubuki, Rahku and Hisashi stared, enraptured by Zenrachi's words, as he continued. "The pain only waits to rear its head, preying on those who suffer, turning them to their demons. There was still truth about the gods left to be uncovered, truth about both the storm and the songbird. And in all of that, maybe my purpose waited to be uncovered as well. I *had* to learn the truth and power behind the storm bird and become a true deity, or return and be the storm of destruction of this land. For now, however, it was time for me to vanish for a while. Unsure of how I would escape the Contessa, I had to keep moving and constantly watch my back, knowing that I'd come too far to turn back now. The best place I could think to hide was Kenzai Mountain, for it was sacred ground. But I was far from there, and with a sadistic hothead soon to be on my tail."

Rahku nodded his understanding. "Go on."

"It was around a year ago when a dark cloud formed over Kenzai Mountain. As the rain started to pour, I knew a soul was approaching the top where I hid. I emerged from the cave amidst the heavy downpour, ready to face the Contessa. Instead, I ended up pummeling my knucklehead friend and Yyolin-sensei's kid. You know the rest. Since then we've been crossing names off the list of the Tsurasu. There are few agents left from back then. And the only one we have any connection with now, of those who might know how to stop Yogen's plan... the only one who can help us..."

"Let me guess." Rahku raised an eyebrow. "The crazy one that's out to get us, with bombs to match her 'great' personality. Zen, there's no way-"

"She can help us beat Yogen. She knows Arashi Tochi like the back of her hand."

"And you just happen to have a thing for her," Hisashi muttered, rolling his eyes.

"Such sentiment will only complicate things, making me unable to make the hard choices that I must with the power of a deity," Zenrachi said.

"… So, you're not saying that you don't?" Rahku asked suspiciously after a long pause.

"You're completely missing the point!" Zenrachi shouted at him, flustered.

"So let's see, there's the remaining members of the Tsurasu that we're going to run into sooner or later…" Rahku began.

"Yeah, I can't wait to meet more of your 'work friends'", Hisashi said sarcastically.

"Then there's the madwoman on the loose, a power hungry man searching for magical gems trying to start a new world order based on combat, and a counterpart deity to the one that's in Zen, the song bird, that's bound to show up in the middle of all this. Did I miss anything?" Rahku folded his arms.

"And which part of Ancient Deities and Utopias would you like to begin with?" Zenrachi said, glaring at him.

"The cave atop Kenzai Mountain might be a start. Those markings could make a lot more sense this time around, and perhaps provide us with some answers about the true nature of the storm bird and the stones," Rahku suggested calmly. "And then there's…. Sensei. She probably knows a lot about this stuff."

"Right… *her*. I hate to admit this, but I still fear her reaction at my reappearance."

Rahku shrugged. "It can't be helped. For now, we should head back to Dentori and cross that path when we get to it."

"It would still be best if people were unaware of my return," Zenrachi pointed out. "If the upper region, far from our small village of Suzuma, caught wind of it, it could cause certain… issues for all concerned."

"What makes you so sure of that?" Rahku asked.

"No one cared who I was on my uphill battle as I fought to become a champion. I was overlooked at every turn until one day, finally, my skill was acknowledged. Soon after, they turned me into some symbol of their prosperity in order to lift *themselves* higher. They put me some false pedestal, like a deity itself." Zenrachi shook his head, disgusted. "The people seeing a ghost like me again would only complicate things. I left Dentori for a reason – to do you and the rest of them a favor. Dentori could implode if they knew anything about what the Tsurasu have been doing behind the scenes all this time. The Tsurasu could even try to take over Dentori during the chaos. Don't forget, Yogen is still around, and too unpredictable towe don't know what or how many strings he's really pulling in Arashi Tochi. He has eyes everywhere… and he knows what lies hidden within me. He'd do anything, anything at all, to get to this power, including putting a big target on Dentori."

"What about Garin, the lord of Dentori?" Hisashi asked.

"You mean the lord of *upper* Dentori," Zenrachi retorted

"What do you mean?" asked Rahku.

"Let me ask you something, Rahku. When was the last time you actually saw Garin in Suzuma?"

A long pause greeted Zenrachi's question.

"That's what I thought. If it comes down to it, Suzuma will be the first line of defense of a war that is not theirs to wage. The lord is only there to preserve his so-called empire he's turned that district of Dentori into. We always get the relayed bullshit messages of hope from the captains of the hunters of Dentori, while he sat back and watched us fight for our very existence. And guess who's made it up to the right hand of the captain now?"

"Aure... cala?"

"Aurecala," Zenrachi confirmed. "I never wanted her to become a hunter, but given the way things unfolded, I can't blame her. The good thing is that Cala's skills have drastically improved since our last scuffle, and as far as we know, she's free of the council's influence. We need to keep her on our side."

"Oh, I'm sure you can *convince* her," Rahku said, raising his brows suggestively.

"Meanwhile, the other nation's leaders are nothing more than puppets to the Tsurasu – the ones who are really in control. They're down a few members, but are a very real threat now that Horaiu's existence is known. Dentori could well be in danger…"

"Not to mention-"

"The Contessa. I know," Zenrachi stopped Rahku before he could finish. "She's either going to show up and kill every last one of us, or wait it out and make us come to her. For now, we should keep our course set on Kenzai Mountain," he concluded. He looked up toward the sky, eyes gazing at the moon. "So. It's time to go back to the land of lightning…"

Made in the USA
Lexington, KY
20 December 2019